at home anywhere

mary hoffman

at home anywhere

mary hoffman

new
Winner of the Many Voices Project
Number 120

©2010 by Mary Hoffman
First Edition
Library of Congress Control Number: 2009938594
ISBN: 978-0-89823-250-9
MVP Number 120
Cover and interior design by Mandee Nyhus

The publication of *At Home Anywhere* is made possible by the generous support of the Jerome Foundation and other contributors to New Rivers Press.

For academic permission please contact Frederick T. Courtright at 570-839-7477 or permdude@eclipse.net. For all other permissions, contact The Copyright Clearance Center at 978-750-8400 or info@copyright.com.

New Rivers Press is a nonprofit literary press associated with Minnesota State University Moorhead.

Wayne Gudmundson, Director
Alan Davis, Senior Editor
Managing Editors: Donna Carlson, Suzzanne Kelley
Thom Tammaro, Poetry Editor
Kevin Carollo, MVP Poetry Coordinator
Liz Severn, MVP Fiction Coordinator
Publishing Interns: Samantha Jones, Nancy Swan, Sean Templeton
At Home Anywhere Book Team: Heather Ehrichs Angell, Melissa Barnes,
    Devin Berglund, Noah Bicknell, LeAnn Bjerken, Nazrin Jahangirova
Editorial Interns: Heather Ehrichs Angell, Melissa Barnes, Devin Berglund,
    Noah Bicknell, LeAnn Bjerken, Caitlin Fox, Jenny Hilleren,
    Allison Hesford, Nazrin Jahangirova, Samantha Jones, Tiegen Kosiak,
    Julie Larson, Andrew Olson, Derrick Paulson
Design Interns: Heather Donarski, Morgan Hoyt, Bryan Murphy, Mandee Nyhus
Allen Sheets, Art Director
Fran Zimmerman, Business Manager

Printed in the United States of America

New Rivers Press
c/o MSUM
1104 7th Avenue South
Moorhead, MN 56563
www.newriverspress.com

For my parents,

Fred and Frances Hoffman

Heartfelt thanks to finalist prose judge of the 2008 MVP Competition Leif Enger; as well as New Rivers Press editor Alan Davis, managing editors Donna Carlson and Suzzanne Kelley, and designer Mandee Nyhus. Thanks also to Melissa Barnes and the other members of the *At Home Anywhere* book team: Heather Ehrichs Angell, Devin Berglund, LeAnn Bjerken, Noah Bicknell, and Nazrin Jahangirova for their helpful suggestions. I will always consider them all exceptionally Brave, Young, and Handsome (to borrow from Mr. Enger) for their work on this book.

I'm grateful to the members of the Mumbles writing group (Norm Scott, Vicky Oliver, Vinny Senguttuvan, Holly Hagan, Bruce Bowman, Phyllis Smith, Gina Caulfield, Ina Clare, and Alexis Davis) for their thoughtful reading of the stories in this collection. I'm in debt to Maurice Baudin Jr., who taught creative writing at New York University, to Barbara Friedberg for her support, and to my wonderful daughter for her insight and encouragement. Finally, I tip my hat to Clare and the other members of The Five Gs, the band that launched so many creative careers.

table of contents

flat earth society
........................page 1

moths
..............................page 15

at home anywhere
..................page 35

felix and adauctus
..................page 55

Flat earth society

To anyone who thinks it's got to be bad enough to be fifty-six years old and four months unemployed, Bill Roubideau would like to say *guess again*. They have to go and put the welfare office in Coney Island. To anyone who's been buying the hype about Coney Island "recovering" to the point where middle-class people are going to start rolling in there with kids in the back of their SUVs like it's some kind of *Disneyland*, he'd like to say *keep dreaming*. And to anyone who might have bet that he'd wind up standing in the rain in Coney Island waiting for the welfare office to open at this stage in his life, he'd like to offer his congratulations: *you must be psychic*. On TV and in the papers the reporters acted like it was news that all the decent jobs were going overseas, but even before his accident Bill hadn't felt like he had any kind of job security in years.

The line is a mix of white, Spanish, and black people. There's an SUV parked at the curb with Chinese people sitting inside. After a few minutes they send somebody out to stand in line for the group. That's the way the Chinese are, very group oriented. That's why they're still

at home anywhere

hanging on to communism when just about everybody else in the world that had it has kicked it to the curb. The smell of food reaches Bill a few seconds after the van door opens. They're eating take-out in there. Sitting in a late-model SUV while they eat take-out, and waiting for the welfare office to open so they can apply. To anyone who sees something wrong with this picture, Bill Roubideau would like to say *the line forms here*.

Of course, even the Chinese aren't as communistic as they used to be. The whole week the nightly news has opened with pictures from a town over there where a mud slide buried a school. Nearly all the children inside died. Now the parents were showing up at the site with signs that asked why the school was the only building in the area to collapse. They cried when they talked to reporters. Some of them held up pictures of the kids. You could tell from the poses they were school pictures, and Bill had noticed that most of the kids weren't that good looking. Faces only a mother could love. But he had to agree that probably the worst thing that could happen to anyone was losing a kid. Even though he'd never had any, that he knew of.

A demonstration like that in China was something new. Before, if any of those parents had showed up asking questions and talking to reporters, they would have been shipped off to brainwashing camp. At first watching the reports he'd thought, *poor bastards*, like it couldn't happen here, but you only had to remember Katrina to realize that the story was really the same everywhere. In Katrina they just bussed the people out after the devastation, and left it to them to find their way back if they could. *Fat chance.*

A skinny guard in a blue suit finally beckons them in. Spanish guy. Nice looking, mid-thirties. And like Bill does all the time now, as he walks past the guard he asks himself, *would I take that job?* He thinks he'd go crazy, all day long telling people: "Stand on this line, you're on the wrong line, you should be on that line." But the Spanish guy is working. He's got health benefits and a regular paycheck. What does Bill have? *Don't answer that.*

The same guard stays with them all the way upstairs, into the elevators and out onto the second floor. At the end of a long hallway they come out in an open area where a lot of plastic chairs are set up facing a counter. The way the guard talks to them while he is showing them where to go and when to stop makes Bill feel like he's being processed for jail.

flat earth society

Which is not mean or harsh like you might expect. More like the guard knows he's dealing with a group of people who don't have a clue to what they're in for. It's the KISS treatment: Keep it Simple, Stupid. And yes he knows what that's like because a long time ago back home he got into a fight in a bar. Not for the first time, but unfortunately that time there was a bat handy and he used it. The other guy was in a coma for two weeks, and Bill served six months. *So who suffered more, he still wanted to know?*

On the way past the counter he hears somebody on the phone, but the counter is too high to see the person. He can tell it's a female and that she's black. He tries not to make any assumptions from those facts, but it's not easy. He reminds himself that where he comes from the people are sweeter, black or white, they just are. Up here it's a different story. He'd swear all the races drank rude juice before leaving the house in the morning. *All* the races, so that meant he wasn't prejudiced, right? Unless you could say that he was prejudiced against northerners and leave it at that.

Bill is one of the first people in the line outside, and the guard does a pretty good job of maintaining that order on the way upstairs, so he doesn't have to wait too long before it's his turn. Two Spanish people have just left after their consultation and are still carrying on in that language. He eases up to the counter and starts to explain how he got hurt washing out bottles so he could store leftovers in them. The accident didn't happen on the job so he couldn't get workers' comp, but he was cut bad enough that he hasn't worked in months. The glass severed a tendon in his right hand. His hammer hand. The woman doesn't think to ask him if he was drinking when he was washing out the bottles, and he doesn't volunteer that information. Bill is always, *always* polite because that is how he was raised and he feels like he has to set an example for the people up here, but before he can get the whole story out she says, "Stop!" Stop? He didn't hear her tell the people who went before him to stop, and neither of them was a native speaker of the language. Her face is puffy and she's wearing a wig that doesn't fit right. She looks like hell in fact, but somehow she is in a position to tell *him* to stop.

"I don't need all that information now," she adds, like that was something Bill should already know. She slaps a form onto the counter. "Fill this out. See what it says here? Don't leave anything blank. That means don't leave *anything* blank."

He's still trying to show her how it *ought* to be done. "This for me?" he says, smiling, to show her that despite her attitude he's not about to forget *his* manners. "Thanks, thanks a lot. Where should I bring it when...?"

"Hold up, hold up," she says; "You're just one person. All these people got stories to tell. I'm not the right one to tell them to. Listen to me: fill this out. Don't leave anything blank. Put it in this basket when you're finished. You'll be called."

If her aim is to humiliate, it works. At one stage in his life, yeah, if there had been a bat handy, he might just have used it. He isn't proud of the impulse, but a bat sure took care of the humiliation problem. As it is, he just looks around to let her know that he could count plenty of witnesses in the immediate vicinity. She doesn't seem impressed, and as he heads back to his seat, he realizes it's probably because she already knows the way everybody's eyes will slide off his as he passes. *You didn't see me here, and I didn't see you.*

Bill glances through the entire form before he starts filling it out. It depresses him to think how some people are answering the questions. *Yes* a teenaged mother lives in my household. *Yes* I have a child with a severe disability. *Yes* I have made one too many bad moves in life and ended up here in the welfare office in Coney Island.

Could be worse. After the incident with the bat everyone decent that was still talking to him wrote him off, and he knew he had to get out. People teased him when he told them his plans: *Ain't you leaving that a little late?* Most people were in their twenties when they made their big move, and he was well past that. But Bill knew he'd never get clean if he didn't quit New Orleans. On the bus ride to New York the scene of his return played constantly in his head: how everybody would stare when he drove back in a late model car with a good looking woman in the front seat to show them all how wrong they'd been. That was twenty-two years ago. He can't even remember the last time he'd tried to picture his homecoming. Now he is two months behind on his rent and couldn't afford the fare home on a Greyhound.

He fills out the form. He doesn't leave anything blank. When he walks up to put the form in the basket he tries to catch the clerk's eye to

flat earth society

smile at her but she keeps her focus on her computer screen. He can see her point. Burnout would come pretty fast in a welfare office. *Everybody's got problems.* Don't waste your time or hers. She's not the person you tell them to.

Back in his seat again he takes a glance around. A few people have kids with them, but they're quiet. Maybe because it's early. Kids might still be sleepy. Or maybe they've caught on to their parents' vibe and realize it's not the kind of day to be calling attention to yourself. Now he sees why the Chinese people with the SUV are here. They all look good, nice clothes, kid's got a video game. But Grandpa's with them too and he looks pretty out of it. Maybe they want to put him in a home. It would probably cost more than the damn SUV parked outside to keep him in one for six months, if they paid for it themselves. All that kind of thing must be free back in China.

Bill remembers seeing photographs of the orphanages over there in a *National Geographic*. They always had a subscription because his mother thought it would help him and his sister do better at school. He remembers one picture that showed a whole wall of babies sitting on potties. They were all fed at the same time too. And they didn't seem to mind. They got used to it, until that was what they liked. That's why the whole family is here with Grandpa to apply for welfare. The other old people in the room are alone or with one other person, usually a middle-aged woman. That's the American way, individualism: *You're not a weakling; you can do it on your own!* And the Chinese are fed the opposite: *You can't do it alone, we have to do it together!* His sister Suzette always hogged the *National Geographic* issues that had anything to do with archeology: mummies, pyramids, old bones. Now she worked for a big oil company, telling them where to dig for oil. Which was another kind of buried treasure when you thought about it, so his mother was right about the *National Geographic*. At least in his sister's case.

Bill liked reading about the Russians. Probably had something to do with all the Russian spies that were in the movies and on television at the time. From Natasha and Boris in *Bullwinkle* to the spies that Emma Peel and Napoleon Solo went up against. For her own reading his mother got the *Readers Digest* condensed books, and one time when he was home sick from school he read one about the last tsar's family. That story hooked

at home anywhere

him: the way Rasputin controlled the mother through the hemophiliac son. The way the tsar's enemies used the fact. He was only a kid, but he picked all that up from that book. His mother was very impressed. That might have been the last time she praised his intelligence, that he can recall.

Bill hasn't seen a *National Geographic* since high school. He wonders if they still run many features about the Russians. He wouldn't be surprised if the government pressured the editors to run those stories back then, just to remind the public who the enemy was. He could remember some of the photographs from those articles too. A picture of a very large woman in a very small bikini at a beach on the Black Sea. Kids up in the Arctic Circle getting light therapy. People lining up for shoes (or bread, or cheese, or vodka) that were all the same. Writers sitting in over-furnished rooms to exchange books they weren't supposed to have. You were meant to look at the pictures and think *that would be awful, I'd never want that.* Now he wasn't sure it sounded so bad. You were never alone; you knew where you belonged; you were guaranteed food and a place to live.

Of course that might be sour grapes talking. He wasn't supposed to end up here, in the welfare office in Coney Island. Not with a father who was the most successful insurance salesmen in six parishes, so good he got a new Cadillac every year. Golf and cocktail parties every weekend. Got on the horn when his son graduated from elementary school and called in a couple of favors so Bill could attend the best Catholic high school in New Orleans despite his poor grades. Old man thought that would protect him from the drugs that were becoming so common. *Wrong!* If anything the Catholic school kids had more, because they had the money to buy more. Bill was smoking weed regularly within a month of starting high school. He started taking pills his senior year. But he'd been drinking since seventh grade.

The priests were regular visitors at the house on Sundays after mass. Father Darcy was his favorite. He liked gin and orange juice or a Tom Collins. Sometimes Bill got the job of bringing around the tray. After his first sip, Father Darcy liked to say: "Now that's fortifying." *Some great example for a kid.* When Bill took the tray back to the kitchen he'd finish what was left in the pitcher his mother used to mix the drinks.

And of course his father was an alcoholic, though nobody ever used that word inside the family. How many times had he come home from school to find Bill Sr. sleeping one off on the couch? But his old man managed to make good despite his addiction. Big house, new cars, entertaining priests. Maybe Bill would have been able to do the same if drinking was his only problem. Coke was the nail in the coffin; he'd like to meet anyone who could say no to coke once they tried it.

There's an elderly man at the counter now who's causing some kind of problem, but Bill is too far away to hear what his complaint is. The guard starts over, but by the time he's reached the counter the argument has ended. The old guy stalks off but the guard remains at the counter, not saying anything, staring at the wall of windows on the other side of the room. All the blinds are half-closed, so there's not much to see. The guard might be skinny, but he looks pretty fit. *There's nothing like a man in a uniform.* The last person Bill heard say that was one of the queens in the Quarter. It was around Mardi Gras, and fake uniforms were everywhere. Bill hadn't exchanged sex for drugs or money for years when the queens started dying, but it spooked him anyway. By the time he left, the public campaigns were in full swing. AIDS for the natives and SIDA for the Mexicans. He put off getting tested until he got to New York anyway, half-believing the result might come out different if he got far enough away from the scene. And then he'd felt so strange when the results came back negative. Almost nostalgic. He'd never get so drunk and stupid again. He'd once let a queen fuck him for a leather jacket. *I'd look better in that jacket than you,* he said; *you know you ought to give it to me.* And the queen said: *That may be true, but right now it's on my back, and if you want it you're going to have to let me ride yours.* He saw it as a dare, and everybody knew Bill Roubideau never walked away from a dare.

He'd never have done it if he wasn't coked up. Something else everybody knew about Bill Roubideau: women were his thing. Business women looking for diversion at the end of some three-day conference. Girlfriends on vacation from their husbands and families back home in dullsville. College girls on spring break. Easy to pick up; easy to drop.

The incident with the bat happened around Mardi Gras too, after days of drinking and drugging. He was eligible for job training when he got out of jail. He had two choices: commercial diving or construction. He

at home anywhere

didn't see himself fixing oil rigs underwater, so he chose the construction program. Construction workers always looked good, didn't they? Of course at the time he was only noticing the young ones. Now he realized how bad the older guys looked — big guts on almost all of them. And they complained all the time about their backs and knees. He still looked pretty good, but he was going to have to start doing sit-ups soon if he didn't want to end up in the same shape. Not that anybody but himself would notice. He hadn't been with a woman in a couple of years. Not since Katrina. He was with someone he met at an AA meeting when that disaster started coming on the news. She was all right at the beginning. But when the story from New Orleans dragged on and on it was like she was *obsessed*. Kept asking him if he didn't want to call his mother to make sure she was all right? He got sick of telling her that if anything happened to his mother his sister would call him. At one point she even offered to buy him a plane ticket so he could go back and help. He said he'd be too upset seeing the destruction up close, but the fact was all he felt when he saw how much of the city had been washed away was relief. He felt sorry for the people who died or lost homes, but deep down he was grateful. Now the place couldn't haunt him anymore. No one would know if he didn't make it back there in a late-model car with a pretty woman in the front seat. Relief and a sense of being on the upside of misfortune for once. If he couldn't live there he didn't care if anybody could.

    The sound of heels in the hallway diverts his attention. A group of Russians walks in. Three guys and a woman. Bill knows they're Russians because their voices drift back to him. The men are all dark, with short hair and black leather jackets over new blue jeans. But he doesn't notice much more about the men because the woman they're with is breathtaking. Her eyes are wide set and her lips are full, two things that he knows from reading a *Time* magazine article are considered beautiful everywhere in the world. Her hair is so pale that it's one shade shy of being any color at all, and long. She sounds like she's complaining to the men about something, but then he thinks there is something about the Russian language that makes all their talk sound a little mournful. The guard points to the counter and she starts forward, with the three men around her like secret service; all they're missing are the wires. She's wearing one of those hats that look like someone used half a bear to

Flat earth society

make it and her coat is some other kind of fur, very white and fluffy. Now the men are speaking, and he thinks their Russian makes them sound like bears. Disappointed bears. Ronald Reagan called them that. He said we shouldn't wake up the bear, or let the bear in, or something like that.

They don't stay too long at the counter. They get a form and start walking toward the chairs. The woman's coat is open, and underneath she is wearing a tight-fitting white sweater, white jeans and thigh-high beige boots. All the prostitutes and trannies in the Quarter had those boots one year. *Do a little dance, make a little love, get down tonight, get down tonight.* She is holding the form like it's a platinum credit card application, and not something full of prying questions to get you to spill your guts about your sorry past. She's tossing her hair and looking around like she's squeezing this visit to the welfare office in between appointments with the hairdresser and her personal trainer. He's starting to get her perfume. He knows he should stop looking at her. He's been in trouble before with people who thought he was coming on to their women, and these guys don't look like they'd think twice about working him over. But he can't help himself. It's like he's starving and she's the first food he has seen in a long, long time.

Then something happens. As the woman approaches Bill's row, the form slips out of her hand and sweeps under his chair. For an instant he feels like he did it, he made the paper fall. He bends down to retrieve it, trying to think of what he can say when he puts it into her hands because all of a sudden he's not feeling so sorry for himself anymore. He's feeling pretty good. He's thinking: *I've pulled women better-looking than her...!* But that doesn't last. As he's reaching for the form he loses his balance. He sways a bit and has to use one hand to brace himself against the floor, and one of the men she's with laughs. Then he wants to stay down there until they go past, but they won't do that unless he returns the form, naturally, so he swings up. "Here you go," he says, falsely cheerful, holding it out to her. His voice sounds a little choked so he clears his throat even though he has nothing else to say. She blinks at him. *Do I need to notice you?* One of the guys sticks out his hand to intercept the form. The woman smiles, faintly. *I am beautiful, aren't I? But I am not for you.*

It's hard keeping his eyes forward after that. He wants to track the Russians' progress through the hall, but if even one of them glances back to find him staring after them the humiliation would be unbearable. So instead he thinks about how the room he's in was constructed: how the cubicles were put together, and ceiling panels hung. From time to time a worker drifts forward from the offices at the rear of the floor to exchange a few words with the woman behind the counter. Before retreating these people gaze out over everyone waiting in the chairs, like judges before a competition begins. They don't say anything — no free evaluations. Finally a door opens in the row of offices off to Bill's right. A woman comes out and fishes around inside the basket. Lifting out an application, she reads the first name.

Bill starts to compose a story he can tell people when he finally goes back to work, about the woman coming to the welfare office in Coney Island wearing thigh-high boots and furs. He will say someone else told him the story so they won't know he'd also had business in the welfare office. At the close of the tale he'd repeat the moral he knew they would draw from the story: *Can you believe that? They learn where the welfare office is even before they can speak the language!* The local boys would appreciate the slur, all those bambinos with their family connections in the union. As though that wasn't another kind of welfare. But there was nothing they liked better than hearing about how the immigrants were ruining the country. Of course they clammed up when the crew included Jamaicans. *Eye-ree.* Whatever the hell that meant. Sometimes he couldn't understand a word the Jamaicans said, but at least they worked, didn't come here and go on welfare.

He supposes the Russians were proof that the end of communism wasn't all it was cracked up to be. Because if getting rid of communism was so great, how come they were all coming here? Maybe everybody was better off before. Bill knows he can't be the only American who misses the old Russia, the place that seemed like a reflection in some kind of magic mirror. Like in one of those children's books he remembers his teachers reading aloud, where everything is just a little off. The hero only realizes he's stepped into the mirror universe when his mother offers him ice cream for lunch and tells him if he finishes every bite he can take a tiny piece of broccoli for dessert. The Russians had been such good rivals in everything — sports, space travel, military. He guesses the way things were going, China was the new rival. Their economy was

flat earth society

booming. Plenty of jobs in China. The next Olympics was going to be there.

The last Olympics Bill could recall in any detail was the one where Olga Korbut won so many medals. He wasn't home much by that time, but for that Olympics he'd stick around to watch. The games were something else his mother thought was educational, so they were always on. His sister loved Olga Korbut, but Bill preferred the other one on the Russian team: the big dark one who never smiled, whose family lived in Ekaterinaberg. That was where the last tsar's family was killed, except maybe for Anastasia. He remembers looking at all the Russian gymnasts to see if any of them resembled the photographs of Anastasia in his mother's condensed book about the last tsar. If she had survived they might not have told her who she really was. They might have decided to let her blend in with the population, marry, have children and grandchildren. One of them could be in the Olympics. Bill always enjoyed the little biographies they did of the Russians during the games, showing the athletes' everyday lives, all bundled up walking through the snow with their families, and then inside their small apartments where they lived crammed in with rugs and sofas and old fashioned lamps. He remembers thinking the rooms looked very cozy. *I wouldn't mind that at all.*

Bill gets called in for his interview. Another black woman, but this one isn't so harsh. He pulls all the hospital paperwork out of his wallet and hands it to her. She frowns while she's glancing through the papers, and he gets a little worried. But then she sighs, and silently folds them up before handing them back, so he figures he's okay. She seems a little skeptical about what he says the union said it could do for him after his injury, which was nothing, but once she gets past that she seems to think he might be eligible for some kind of benefits for a short period of time. She asks him when he thinks he'll be able to work again. Bill tells her that he's been showing up at the hiring hall for the last couple of weeks, but there wasn't anything for him since he still can't grip a tool for more than a minute. She says he needs to get some physical therapy, and also that he has to show up at another city office to be interviewed for a job or training, or he won't continue to get benefits.

"In case you haven't heard, this isn't the old welfare," she says.

He can't tell if she thinks the change is an improvement or the worst

at home anywhere

thing to ever happen in her line of work. She tells him that once he's approved he'll get a benefits card instead of a check: "The stores where you can shop have machines, and you swipe the card in that and then you type in your number."

He says, "Sounds like a credit card," trying to make a joke to show his appreciation for what she is doing for him, getting him set up. He grovels a little bit, humiliates himself, for no good reason. She doesn't appreciate the effort.

"Not really," she says, wearily. So that's that.

When he gets outside her office, he looks around, but he doesn't see the Russians. His first impulse is to wait to see if they come out of one of the other rooms where the interviews are held. But in this kind of place someone might ask him to move on since his business is completed, and he doesn't want the woman to see that. So he leaves, finding his way back to the elevators and downstairs where the guard who let him in earlier is talking with another guard. There's a clock on one wall and Bill is shocked to see that he's only been inside the place an hour. An hour and ten minutes ago he would have seen that as a positive, but now he wishes the process was a little less efficient if it meant he could see the Russians again.

The rain has stopped. Bill decides to go up on the boardwalk before walking to the subway to take a look out at the water. It's not like he gets down here that often, and he doesn't plan on coming back again real soon. Not if he can help it.

The boardwalk is in pretty rough shape. It looks like someone's taken an axe to it, splintered everywhere and big chunks missing in every direction as far as he can see. He picks his way over the gaps to the railing. The beach isn't completely deserted: there's a man with a dog, and another man without one. He looks out at the water, gray green and calm today, not a lot of breakers. A container ship, far out on the horizon.

The view reminds him of a writer he'd seen on TV a few days earlier, promoting a new book. Something called *The Earth is Flat*. This was on channel thirteen, so Bill knew better than to think the writer had missed the social studies lesson about the mistaken belief people once had that ships would sail off the edge of the world if they went too far from home.

Flat earth society

But he was curious about what the writer did mean, so he paused to listen. It turned out that all he meant was that if somebody in India can do your job cheaper than you can, and if your company fires you and hires him, then somehow that is good news for everybody. That was his theory, the flat earth theory.

Now Bill looks out and tries to make himself see the horizon as a kind of drop-off point. He can't do it; you can't forget what you know, *you can't stop progress.* He guesses that's as true for the Russians as anyone else. They can't go back to what they were before. And we can't go back to having them that way. That's when he thinks he understands what the writer on TV was talking about, maybe better than anyone in that studio or anyone listening at home. He ought to write his own damn book. His book would say: It's true, the earth is flat now, really really flat, because in China the children get buried in mud after somebody looks the other way when their school is constructed, and in New Orleans the levees break, and the Russians are here with us, down in Coney Island at the welfare office. That's the real flat earth society.

Bill heads back to the staircase. He's looking down at the boardwalk to avoid stepping into a hole so he doesn't see the Russians until they're just about to come over the top. There's no time to adjust his stride and he ends up face to face with the woman on the top step. Automatically, his standard reaction to such encounters kicks in: *I was born here, why should I be the one to move?* But she yields and steps around him. Shamed, he shifts; they end up facing each other again. She laughs and he smells her cosmetics. They are the expensive kind, even warmed by her breath they smell fresh and light. *Empty my pockets, take all I have.*

One of the Russians bumps into him and he steps aside. They've already moved off a few steps when he hears himself say, "Why don't you lose that trash and come with me?" He says it the way he would have in a club at Mardi Gras, half joking but half serious, and up until the last couple of years before he left, it worked. Believe it or not, it worked, more times than you would imagine, with all kinds of women: the ones in town for conventions, the ones on package vacations; all eager for an adventure so they'd have something to tell their friends when they got home.

One of the bears wheels around to look at him and snarls something. He'd welcome a punch; hell, he'd rather go down fighting. But the

at home anywhere

woman makes an appeal and they turn away. *He's no threat.* He steps after them, frantic to say something that will bring them back.

"Hey — mother fuckers!"

Now all of them turn around at once. The woman's forehead creases into two soft rolls and he can hear that mournful voice trying to draw them off.

"Hey, why don't you fuckers go back to Russia where you belong!"

One of them is coming for him; he's forgotten how fast an angry man can close in. The first punch lands. He staggers back. *This is more like it.* He tries to keep the woman in his sights, *Anastasia*, pleading for his life. Another punch and he's falling, his brain reeling with the effort to find the words that will make them stay angry enough to beat him senseless, the flat earth rising up to meet him on his way down.

moths

"You made me look very Asian," Beth said. She was standing beside Brian's easel, wearing the shiny robe she put on during breaks from posing. All the other students in Katherine's pastel portraiture class had left their work to gather in the corner where the coffee was set out.

Beth didn't wait for Brian to respond before going on.

"I wish I could show this to the Vietnamese guy I'm seeing. His father was an American soldier, so he's a mutt, like me. He was in an orphanage for a long time and then he ran away. He was like, eight years old or something, and he decided to just walk out of Vietnam. He had to go through Cambodia. At one point some Vietnamese soldiers captured him. They thought he was with some really evil Cambodian leader? They tortured him. They put him in this metal box and threw rocks at it. His ears bled."

In the past, the model's chatter hadn't bothered Katherine. But now, with David moving around upstairs, she wished Beth was quieter.

at home anywhere

"Pol Pot," Katherine said, moving to Brian's other side. "That could be who the soldiers were looking for." Given Beth's age, it was possible she had never seen the photographs of skulls piled up all around Cambodia. Or perhaps she had seen them and forgotten or confused them with photos of horrors in other places.

Katherine knew her remarks might not be welcome. She had called a break and the students were entitled to a rest from instruction. But she felt a duty to enlighten the younger woman. Beth ought to know the name of that "really evil leader" if she meant to tell the story again.

To Katherine's pleased surprise, Beth looked interested. "Pol Pot? I'll ask Dinh if that's who they were looking for. He told me his mother's family was related to some powerful people, but they still had to leave the country when the Americans did. I think they went to Thailand though, not Cambodia." Beth spoke matter-of-factly while delivering her boyfriend's biography, but it was obvious that using his name in conversation was still a novelty. Katherine remembered that sensation — when speaking a new lover's name was like holding him in your mouth.

"Don't you want some coffee, or a cookie?" she asked, directing the prompt at both Beth and Brian, but more concerned about her student. He'd nodded politely all through Beth's monologue, but only looked her way once or twice. The rest of the time he gazed intently at his work, dabbing at it with a chamois cloth. He was the only male in the class and was younger by two decades than the rest of the students. Those factors probably explained his continuing reluctance to join the others around the coffee table. Though it was often the case that newer students stayed with their work during the breaks, as if eager to make up for lost time.

"Maybe I will take a cup," Brian replied, sheepishly. He glanced sideways at Beth to make sure she wouldn't be offended if he didn't stick around to hear more about her boyfriend. Laying the chamois aside, he moved to join his classmates.

"Beth?"

"No thanks. I'm trying to cut back. I was getting headaches."

"Help yourself to a cookie then," Katherine murmured, and finally Beth drifted toward the refreshments.

Katherine went to the opposite end of the space, seemingly to put away the clay head she'd used earlier to demonstrate the muscles that lay under the skin. In fact she wanted to listen for any sounds coming moths

from the apartment overhead. David had begun to stir during the final minutes of the last pose. Was there something different about his tread? No — it seemed as purposeful as ever.

Today was the last of the four Saturday morning sessions in the portraiture workshop. Katherine had come close to canceling this last meeting. Her ex-husband had flown up from Raleigh two days earlier for a series of medical tests. Of course there were doctors in Raleigh, but when David called to explain why he was coming to New York, she suppressed the impulse to remind him of the fact. He said he was starting to forget things. "We all do that," Katherine replied. "I don't," he answered, curtly.

With anyone else it would have been natural to ask, "What kinds of things are you forgetting? Names and dates? Or, finding yourself behind the wheel on the highway, why you left the house, and where you are going?" But he had not sounded ready to share such details, and she decided to leave the questions to the doctors. It turned out he had already seen his internist – an old family friend. "And what does he say?" Katherine had asked, the night David arrived. "He's talking Alzheimer's, strictly as a rule-out, but I want to get a couple of other opinions. He's good, but he's a small-time guy. Forty-hour work-week guy and likes it that way."

He hadn't questioned her decision to accompany him to the first appointment here in the city. He didn't like making a fuss or being the object of one, but she could tell he was grateful. She supposed strangers would find their relationship odd, but their divorce hadn't been rancorous. They'd agreed to raise their son jointly as far as possible, though he would live with his mother until he was ready for college. To maximize Geoff's access to his father during those years they decided that whenever work brought David to New York, he would stay with them. Geoff's time in Oberlin made a break in the routine, but they resumed the practice when their son returned to New York after graduating to try to have a music career. By that time the marriage David had left Katherine for was long over.

The students drifted back to their easels. Katherine didn't think they would have minded if she'd called them by Thursday, or even Friday, to let them know they wouldn't meet as usual on the weekend. They were all veterans of past workshops, and knew she would make up the time.

at home anywhere

In the end she decided it might be best to finish out the class so she wouldn't have to worry about scheduling an extra session. Anyway, that fit better with her long-range plans; she'd had it in mind for some time to take a break from teaching. Geoff's move south had prompted the notion that she might sell the brownstone and buy something smaller. She meant to start looking for a suitable space once she put this workshop behind her. She would still need a studio for her own work and her classes. The sooner she was resettled, the sooner she could offer them again.

Margaret, a quiet woman in her late sixties who'd been a judge before retiring, started forward from the rear of the studio with Beth in her wake. The table Katherine used for framing her work was located directly behind Margaret's easel, and she moved toward it now, ready to stage a rescue should her student begin to show signs of wearying of the model's flood of talk.

The new boyfriend was still the younger woman's topic.

"Dinh is so amazing. He does so many things so well. Right now he's supervising this hotel construction job in the East Village? He's in charge of the whole site, even though he's younger than some of the other guys. What he really wants to do is go back to Vietnam someday to help build it up. He could really be helpful there, because he knows how to do so much stuff from scratch. Like, even though he knows how to build a house with power tools, he can do it with hand tools too. So it wouldn't be a problem if he went somewhere where they didn't have electricity? He told me that when he was a little boy he and his friends used to make their own balls to play with. They'd go out into the forest and get the rubber from the trees and then they'd bring it back and cook it. After that they had to roll it into a ball, but first they had to find someone in the village with a really flat table to roll it on. They'd take turns rolling the ball around the table until it was perfectly round. If there was even the smallest imperfection in the table, the ball wouldn't be round, and then they couldn't use it — it would bounce all crazy. That's what's so amazing about him: he can look at almost anything and tell you how to make it from scratch."

Katherine had been going through the motions of measuring a print she wanted to frame when Beth's anecdote prompted her own revelation and she found herself speaking,

"That reminds me of a time in Indonesia when I wanted to buy my

moths

son a ball. The company told us we had to have servants. I thought I might have two; someone to help inside the house and someone to take care of the garden, but they said no, you need more, all these people depend on us for jobs, so it's good for community relations. They said I wasn't to walk to the store. If I wanted something, the driver had to take me. That day, on the way to get the ball, the driver told me that when he was a child he went through the same process: going out to get the rubber, and making it into a big sheet, and then going through all those steps you described. He took me to just the right place when we got to the market. I remember riding home holding the ball in my hand like it was some kind of rare pearl."

She had said "the driver" but the regular driver didn't take her that day. The head gardener filled in for him. Not that he did any gardening, not directly. Soon after they arrived in the country he had presented himself to fill that role, on the recommendation of one of David's colleagues at the bank. Before long he was master of their domestic operations; educating his new employers about what needed to be done to maintain an expatriate household, coordinating the work of all the other people who came into their employ, many of whom seemed to be relations. She often had the impression that he concealed the full extent of the problems that arose among the staff, feeling sure she heard only a small fraction of what went on behind the scenes. He might ask permission for his niece to take a month off to go to stay with her cousin who was getting married, or for a nephew to travel home to bury his mother; easy applications to consent to when there was always another niece or nephew to take the absent one's place.

To her surprise, she couldn't immediately recall his name. At one time, she must have used it a dozen times a day. She felt its shape somewhere in her memory, but her conscious mind could not recover it. Was this the kind of forgetting that had prompted David to visit the doctor?

The timer went off, signaling the end of the break. Margaret smiled and nodded at Katherine, who felt herself blush. She didn't usually talk about herself during classes — perhaps Beth's confessional prattle was rubbing off on her! Or, more likely, her concern about David had upset her more deeply than she'd realized.

Beth climbed onto the stage and resumed her pose. As Katherine went from student to student, suggesting and reminding, she saw herself setting out on the shopping trip for the ball, seated in the middle of the back seat of the blue Lincoln, one arm across Geoff. They had moved slowly along the road between the American compound and the center of town. The grounds around the compound were so very green, and sometimes ripe fruit dropped from the trees as the car trundled past. There were times when she had been afraid on that road, especially as it neared the shopping district, where the streets were always thronged with traffic. There was political trouble in the country during those years. But that day, the day the head gardener took her, she wasn't afraid at all.

Something fell upstairs. Momentarily, she listened more acutely, and heard David moving toward the side of the kitchen where the sink was. She thought he must have spilled something. In the past he would have known where to get what he needed to clean up the mess. He seemed to find her home suddenly unfamiliar, however. He had become careless about picking up after himself as well. The day before she'd come upon his cigar paraphernalia, the lid to the humidor left open, the clipper and an uncut cigar abandoned alongside. A room away a chess set had been taken down, but only a handful of pieces had been placed on the board, and not in their correct locations. An odd assortment of canned food sat atop the kitchen counter; nothing that, in combination, would have made a snack or dish: evaporated milk, diced tomatoes, baking soda.

She had reached Jo's easel. Jo taught art at one of the local private schools, and was quite skilled. "This is coming along very nicely. You might want to check that line," she said, pointing past Jo's shoulder to the place where Beth's neck met her head. "I think it's a bit shorter than that."

P— the head gardener's name began with the letter P. Katherine remembered how kind he was the day she came home from her batik class with her first finished piece. She laid out the fabric on the dining room table along with her canting tools. They looked like smoking pipes, only the vessel atop the handle held wax instead of tobacco. The gardener came upon her there. "Come see my batik," she said, intending to perform a kind of dress-rehearsal for him, to practice what she would say to David later that day. P— seemed surprised to learn that she had taken a class, and then plainly pleased. He said that his father had worked in a batik factory, and that her piece was very good for a beginner.

moths

That was the start of warmer relations between them. From the moment Katherine arrived in Indonesia, she had tried to forget the advice printed in the handbook the bank provided newcomers to help them transition into life abroad. The book was filled with warnings: about locking up valuables, and the importance of avoiding personal conversations with household staff. The instructions for discouraging the solicitation of personal information suggested that if ignoring the questioner didn't work, one could pick up a newspaper and begin reading, or pretend to make a telephone call. She remembered sitting up in bed their first night in the country, giggling as she read that recommendation aloud. When she finished David agreed that it all seemed ridiculous, but then added: "Still, I have heard stories, so you probably do need to be a little more careful than you'd be at home. Whoever put that book together wanted to help people avoid bad situations, so I wouldn't discount it completely."

At least he didn't insist that she become part of the clique of bank wives who filled their days with shopping when they weren't visiting each other and drinking. She knew there were a few who threw themselves into charity work, but that wasn't her inclination, either. She had Geoff to look after, and her batik classes. And then the sympathy she felt growing between herself and P— filled in for what other company she might have lacked. She took to showing him all her pieces as they were completed.

She also showed him the single page devoted to batik in her college art history book. It stated that batik clothing was compulsory at the seventeenth century Javanese court. One of the prescribed colors was the rich brown dye that came from the Soga tree. P— added much to the textbook description. He identified the Sawat motif pictured in the illustrations, which reminded Katherine of a weeping willow, as the vehicle on which Vishnu traveled. The Padang Rusa design that she purchased from her teacher was said to have protected an early Javanese prince from death. Her first effort was an imitation of the Kopi Pecah pattern, which contained the lesson that the individual should always be ready to sacrifice for the common good.

One afternoon she had an appointment with a dealer who sold antique batik and she had the sudden inspiration to ask P— to go with her. At first she thought he misunderstood the request. He said he would be glad to give the driver directions to that shop, and the others he knew of that traded in old batik. Katherine repeated her request, expanding on the very practical reasons he ought to accompany her. He could help her determine if the pieces she was shown were authentic, and whether the prices being asked for them were reasonable. The latter argument convinced him: it was his duty to lend her his expertise. That day she found two beautiful pieces that he said were very valuable. After that, he took over the driving responsibilities on all her batik-buying expeditions, and joined her in talking to the sellers. He was always careful to maintain a certain formality during the outings. But when they were finished, and she was seated behind him in the car again, moving through the crowded streets in the center of town toward the compound, she tried to prolong their conversation. Did he guess that the effort was partly for external consumption? To show the people who saw them that they were no ordinary pairing of corporate wife and Indonesian servant, that it was possible to cross those boundaries and have real dialogue? But as they drew closer to the neighborhood where the bank's employees lived, the answers P— gave grew shorter and shorter, and finally she accepted his reluctance and stopped speaking. He might be concerned that someone would see how easy they were with each other, and start a rumor that there was something inappropriate about their relationship. His reputation was important: Katherine would move on in a few years time, and after that he would need his good name to find a job with another family.

She was pleased when he began asking favors of her, seeing that as a sign of his growing trust. Would she consent to speaking with his niece, who was finishing a social work course, and wanted to work for an American missionary group? And after that meeting had taken place, would she write a letter of reference? He began to let her know whenever a family member had given birth, and she understood the news as a prompt to bundle whatever clothes Geoff had already outgrown to donate to the new mother and child. She gave them happily, and even included some things Geoff might still be wearing, as further evidence of how much she valued their friendship

It was quiet overhead. David must have gone back upstairs to the bedroom. Or he might be sitting at the table, reading the paper. She had only consented to accompany him overseas when he was offered his first international posting because of the opportunity the trip presented

moths

to try some of the art forms she'd learned about in her classes. That was heaven: to sit in a darkened room and look at slides of Hindu bronzes, Mayan temple paintings, and Ashanti clay heads. After arriving in Indonesia, she had briefly considered learning to make the shadow puppets the country was justly famous for, but the batik process was more intriguing. Errors weren't easily disguised. Oil paint could be almost endlessly wiped and reworked, but the same flexibility wasn't possible with batik. Once wax spilled on the wrong part of the cloth it was almost certainly ruined. Scraping was possible, but not often successful. Even after boiling the fabric retained some traces of the wax. That was equally true for finished pieces, and was the source of the textile's unique odor, still faintly noticeable in the curtains around the dressing room down here in the studio, and all the throw pillows in the rooms upstairs, and the trunk full of hand-dyed fabric at the foot of her bed.

She had come around to Margaret's easel. "Be careful not to overwork," she murmured, passing on. They had lived in Indonesia three years before being transferred to Turkey, where she studied with a master papermaker. A short, thickset man, with exceptionally hairy arms and wrists, and a large, pock-marked nose. He could drop a few dots of oil paint into a water bath, turn them with a stroke of a stick, and when he pulled the paper waiting at the bottom of the tray up through the paint, tulips appeared. He smoked. "I only smoke for my health," he'd explain, puffing away in the courtyard outside his studio. "It cleans the blood." He laughed at her objections, as though human biology was different in Turkey, and research findings didn't apply. What would she do with all the work she had produced while traveling? If she moved into a smaller space she would have to put a lot of it in storage. Or give it to Geoff. If — when Geoff married, his wife would decide what to display, if anything. Then his children would inherit the work. But it was doubtful anyone would value it as Katherine did.

Brian's easel was next. He needed more direct instruction than the others, and she stopped longer at his side. She had him pick up the kebab skewer she handed out to all her students on the first day of any class, reminding him of how it could be used to check the dimensions of his drawing against Beth's anatomy, and asked him to reexamine the relative lengths of her upper and lower arms. Under her instruction Brian had become less tentative with each class, but today she was glad he had drawn those parts of the portrait so lightly. The correction would not be too obvious.

One afternoon on their way back from a batik workshop, where she had purchased some antique pieces, she began to imagine what it would be like to be married to P—. That day, as usually happened when they entered a gallery, the salespeople shifted their attention to him once they realized how knowledgeable he was, and that he had the final word on her purchases. They did not ignore her — instead, she was included in their admiring gaze. The same thing happened when she went out with David socially. It was as though people extended the respect they had for the two men to her, for having the wisdom to align herself with such intelligent, effective individuals.

She had no intention of acting on her fantasy, naturally. In fact, the two men complemented each other: she enjoyed each one better because the other was present. Both were powerful and able in their different domains; the men people looked to when there was trouble. One small and slender with a voice like water running over stones. The other tall, powerfully built, and loud in comparison to the local people; almost rude in his dealings with everyone, his seniors at the bank and even his friends. He was gentler with the servants, in deference to her, she was sure; and that pleased her. She made sure that he understood how much P— contributed to the smooth running of their lives, by describing the lengths he went to in order to carry out her instructions. P— went here; P— took care of that problem. And she also made sure that P— knew that her husband had her continuing devotion, by bringing him into their conversations as much as possible. In the batik workshops, discussing color: "My husband likes red; my husband would think this print is too busy." At home discussing menus and calendars: "My husband likes fish; my husband doesn't like curry." She was like Beth, she realized, working some reference to one into every conversation with the other, just for the pleasure of hearing their names.

Then, about halfway through their second year in Indonesia, there was some trouble about a VCR. The company had purchased one for each family so they could watch videos from home, where the machines were enjoying a craze. Katherine had never been a big movie fan, and neither was David, but sometimes colleagues pressed films on him. She could tell from the sudden increase in traffic past the living room while they watched the movies that the servants were fascinated. For the first few weeks after it arrived, she liked to lay a hand atop the VCR upon returning from a batik class or errand. It was usually warm, but she didn't mind if the staff used the machine when she was out of the house as long as the work got done, and she was sure P— would see to that. She didn't say anything, except to tell P— and the nanny that she didn't want Geoff watching.

The day it went missing she didn't notice until the cook came in to ask if Katherine would like a drink before David arrived, and gasped with theatrical horror at the gap on top of the television cart. Katherine wouldn't have cared, but they were due to host a party soon and she knew that David's superiors would expect to see their gift installed in a place of honor; and told what a "lifesaver" it was to have American entertainment in that foreign place.

P— was summoned. To her disappointment his first words were a reminder: did she recall that more than once he had asked if she wanted him to have one of the boys put the VCR in the safe for her?

Did he think she meant to call him to account? Like some ordinary corporate wife who looked for things to blame the servants for? She quickly reassured him: "I don't hold you responsible..." But he wasn't satisfied. "These boys and girls are very poor," he said, "this machine represents a great temptation." She bristled, but held her tongue, and after a moment he went on: "*Nyonya* Walker, I hope you will allow me to look into these matters. Will *Tuan* Walker need to know about this before I have had time to finish my discoveries?"

"Oh, no," she said. "I won't say anything to him at this point." She started to ask, "How long...?" But decided not to, to let P— know he had her blessing to do whatever he thought best, and to take as long as he needed.

That evening David arrived home after dark. He had been out with some recent arrivals from Texas, and went directly upstairs to bed. The next few evenings they were both out, at the various events planned to welcome the newcomers. Katherine was the last to volunteer to entertain

at home anywhere

them, hopeful that by that time the VCR would be returned. But days went by, and P— made no mention of his progress. She told herself that he might have forgotten about the theft in all the preparations for the party. Then, to her shame, as the date neared, the advice in the company brochure came to mind: "If you do discover thieving, don't wait — terminate!" Finally, she noticed that one of the boys who had worked in the kitchen was missing, and she asked P— outright if his absence was related to the missing machine. He admitted that the boy was indeed the thief.

"Did he tell you where the VCR is? The man who gave it to us is coming to the party. I want to be able to show it to him."

P— seemed surprised at the question. "This young man doesn't work here anymore," he repeated.

"That's fine, I'm sure you did whatever was best. But where is the machine now?"

She didn't imagine the coolness of his reply. "I'm very sorry. The young man's father is very, very sick. He took this machine to sell for money for medicine. I told him not to return. For him, this is a serious punishment. So many of the boys and girls have these problems. That is why all visitors are wise to use the safe."

She supposed it had been unrealistic to expect the machine to be returned. But she wished P— had let her know sooner. "Of course," she said, suppressing her annoyance. "Never mind, I'll take care of it."

The next day, she asked the regular driver to take her to the street of electronics shops. She purchased another VCR, same make and model as the one that was stolen. She insisted the shopkeeper give her one that came in a box. She didn't want to imagine that she was buying back her own machine.

David never guessed. His manager was suitably pleased at her display of gratitude when she showed him his gift the night of their dinner party. But later, as she directed one of the houseboys to unplug the machine and carry it upstairs to their bedroom, she silently cursed the giver for introducing a note of discord in her relations with P—. She would have liked to leave the thing unguarded, in hopes that someone else would spirit it away.

Jo's easel was situated nearest the opening to the staircase that led upstairs, and as Katherine started back that way she realized that David was standing in the doorway. That was surprising enough — he had never visited one of her classes — but his expression was equally unnerving. He looked cagey, as though he was aware of the potential for error in such a setting, and was trying to anticipate where the traps might lay.

"David! Come in, please. Are you having trouble finding something? Everyone, this is David, my ex-husband."

He didn't answer, and after a moment stepped into the room, striding forward with his old confidence, as if motion extinguished all his uncertainty, made him forget his forgetting. He didn't stop where she was, however, but kept going to the other side of the ring of easels, and then began to circle, standing half a minute behind each one, and frowning, or nodding in appreciation. She tried to behave as though there was nothing alarming in his slow rotation. But that became more difficult as time went on, and he showed no sign of leaving. Her students seemed pleased at the opportunity to smile their greeting — especially her veterans. They knew something about him: that he'd had an important position at a bank, that they'd traveled and had an amicable divorce, and that his second marriage hadn't lasted. She supposed that even adult students had some curiosity about their teachers' lives outside of school. The more romantic among them might even be imagining that David's appearance heralded the rekindling of their old relationship.

Her own attitude changed, from moment to moment — the sympathy and fear she felt for him one instant giving way to angry resentment the next. At one point she found herself mentally scolding him: *Go away! What do you want here now, so late?* While they were traveling she'd never minded that he hadn't shown great interest in her classes. Or so she'd told herself. She hadn't needed more approbation than his obvious pleasure at hearing the surprise the other executives and their wives expressed when they discovered that the artwork they had been admiring as they stood around the living room with drinks was the product of her own energies. It wasn't until he had asked for a divorce so he could marry someone he'd met in the London office when they were posted there that she began to think he had always been too ready to leave her to herself.

at home anywhere

Brian had stopped working. Instead he busied himself rearranging his pastels; a sign that David had been standing nearby too long. She went to David's side and took his arm. He resisted — but only slightly, and only for a moment. "Come upstairs, I want to show you something," she lied.

He shot her a sharp, wary glance. Said, with some of his old asperity: "That's not necessary. Finish here first. Whatever it is can wait."

She heard some of the students murmur goodbyes as he brushed past them. Then she busied herself at the coffee table while listening to make sure he shut the door at the top of the stairs. The session was almost over. How could she hurry her students out, without offending them? Returning to Jo she said: "That looks ready to spray."

The timer sounded, for the last time. Katherine shut off the spotlights and turned on the overhead lights, then gave the group instructions for how to spray their work to fix the colors. "You can take your pieces outside. Spray evenly, but don't spray the bottom, because I'm going to show you how to sign your work."

She'd always assumed that her health would fail before David's when she gave the matter any thought, which was rarely. In all their years of travel, she couldn't remember him suffering any great distress on account of strange food or water, or missing work because of illness. While it had always taken her weeks to adjust to the local amoebas, and she'd been laid up with what was probably dengue fever once. She hadn't realized until now how much she depended on the notion that he would outlive her. Even after they were divorced it had comforted her to believe that if anything happened to her, Geoff would have David to depend on for years and years to come.

Her students were drifting back to the basement from the garden. Once they were all together again, she demonstrated how to store and protect a pastel, and how to have it framed. "A single mat will keep the glass from touching it, but some people like to use a double mat, with the innermost one cut slightly larger than the one the viewer sees. Over time, even under glass, some of the pastel will fall off, and if you have that recessed double mat, the dust will drop to the innermost one and you won't see it." Then she showed them how to sign their work, her hand shaking a little with the strain of trying to appear unhurried.

They began to pack up their supplies. Brian took longer than the others, and was still at the sink washing his hands when the rest of the group had collected near the door to say goodbye. Jo asked when the next round of classes would begin.

"At this point I'm not really sure," Katherine replied. "I've been thinking about selling this house, so I may spend some time looking for a new place."

"Oh, no! Sell this?" Jo exclaimed, sounding really dismayed; "You'll never find enough room to hold classes anywhere else!" No one else said anything, but they all looked shocked at the announcement.

"I don't think it will be that difficult," Katherine protested, "I haven't really started looking yet, but the realtor I spoke to said it shouldn't be impossible."

Jo looked dubious, but she and the others repeated their thanks and made their way out.

Beth had retrieved her over-sized shoulder bag, and stood looking on while Brian dried his hands. As Katherine approached, lifting the young woman's pay out of her pocket, she heard Beth say: "...the other day I was about to swat a moth that flew out of my closet, and Dinh stopped me. He's Buddhist — you know what they believe, right? Like how all life is connected, and if you do something bad to one creature it's like doing something bad to yourself? He just has so much reverence for anything that's alive. It's so refreshing!"

"I'm sorry to have to hurry you along," Katherine apologized, joining them, "but as you saw I have a guest this weekend, and we have plans this afternoon."

Brian hastened to retrieve his belongings. When that was done he waved at both the women from the doorway. "It was nice to meet you," he told Beth. Then, including Katherine, he went on: "Good luck with everything."

"He's pretty cute," Beth noted, after he left, taking the money Katherine offered, and folding it into a fabric wallet. "I like big noses, sometimes."

"He's very nice," Katherine said, with finality, hoping her tone would staunch the flow of Beth's remarks, but the model went on: "He reminds me of some guys I met a couple of weeks ago. They were from — Afghanistan? No, Azerbaijan. I think that's how you say it. They had big noses and they were really masculine." Then, to cure the quick remorse that must have followed her expression of admiration for any male but Dinh, she added: "Dinh is really masculine, too, but in a different way. He looks delicate, but he's really strong. He can pick me up and hold me over his head for the longest!"

Katherine remembered the Indonesian men, in their long sarongs. Most slighter than she was herself, and graceful — they didn't walk the way American men did. Some of the other company women went so far as to say the Indonesian men seemed feminine, but obviously that was wrong. They were the heads of large families. They fought and killed each other over political and ethnic rivalries.

"When should I come again?"

"Oh — that's right, you were changing when I told the others: I'm not going to offer classes for a while. So at this point I think it's best if I call you when I start again."

"No problem," Beth said, placing the wallet into her bag. Then, to Katherine's surprise, she narrowed her eyes and asked: "Are you all right?"

"Me? I'm fine," Katherine replied, embarrassed at how poorly she had disguised her anxiety. "You know how it is when you have a sudden house guest. My ex-husband only called to say he was coming a couple of days ago. I considered canceling today, in fact, but then I thought better of it."

But Beth's concern had vanished as suddenly as it appeared. Halfway through Katherine's explanation, she began to seem bored, glancing toward the door and shifting on her feet. "Well, take care," she said, disinterestedly, when it was finished, and moved towards the exit.

Katherine followed her out, as far as the areaway in front of the house, and watched her until she reached the rose bushes in the yard three houses away. Then she turned and, moving rapidly, took the two steps down to the studio, locking the gate, and then the door; fighting the urge to run outside and after Beth to ask her to come again the following Saturday, and talk all she wanted, about her boyfriend or anything else. She could get enough students to fill a class by that time. Most of the people who'd just left would sign up. It suddenly seemed unwise to change her routine just then, with David's future so uncertain. Maybe the best course would be to go on exactly as she had been for so many years, holding classes and doing commissions and going to Portrait Society meetings. Forget selling the house. The way to deal with change might be to hold out as long as you could against it.

She started moving the easels out of the way, haphazardly. Someone had left an old shirt behind, paint-stained, and she wondered if the owner would bother coming by for it. Did she want to be found here in her studio as usual, or not? The other way to deal with change would be to break with everything in the old life at once. Stop teaching. Move house. Lose husband. Ex-husband.

Not long after the VCR was lost, their house in Indonesia was infested with moths. If you could call their presence an infestation: they didn't bite or buzz but covered everything like the kudzu that grew alongside the roads around Raleigh. After a day or two of shooing the moths away from anything she wanted to pick up or touch, David came home with a spray can of insecticide. She noted some discomfiture among the servants when he brandished it. And then that evening P— came to warn her. "This spray is not good," he said. "It kills many things. Your husband should not use this." Katherine was pleased that he had come to her with his concerns. Their relationship had still not returned to the easy exchange that preceded the theft. She missed him, and hoped his petition meant that he had forgiven her for her missteps in that situation.

David scoffed when she described the gardener's apprehension. "That's ridiculous," he said. But he went on, and the further explanation was a sign of respect for the other man. He didn't usually bother providing evidence to support his arguments. "The stuff is perfectly safe. They use it at the bank."

"I don't know if that's saying much," she murmured, but she didn't try to stop him later that night when everyone was in bed, and he went through all the downstairs room, spraying. Why not, when she was trying to restore her dealings with P— to their old ease?

At first, she had explained away the seeming contradiction as an exercise in comparison. The cautiousness that P— demonstrated threw her husband's energy into high relief. Showed her she had chosen well: whatever the problem, her husband acted, and accepted complete responsibility no matter the result. But there was another reason for her failure to stop him from using the spray; shameful and unacknowledged until long after they had left the country: the small, small voice of resentment that had started speaking to her as P— withdrew his companionship after the theft, that even the promise of renewed friendship couldn't entirely dispel. Who was he to judge her, the voice asked; and how unfair he was to give up on her after one mistake!

The next morning the moths were gone. The servants must have swept them out of the house before anyone in the family was up, because only a few of their carcasses remained, in the corners of the rooms or shelves, and there had been so many. No one said anything about the matter until a few days later, when P— came to her as she worked in her studio. He was cradling something in his hand. One of the lizards that were everywhere in Indonesia, and that everyone tolerated because they ate insects. It was dead. "You see," he said, "this comes from the spray."

"I'm sorry," Katherine said. "I'll tell my husband. You know the way he is — stubborn. But next time, I promise, I'll stop him." He didn't say anything, but she knew she had lost his trust. She felt deeply sad, and regretted that she hadn't tried harder to convince David. The opportunity to prove her good intentions about using the spray never came — the moths did not appear again.

She had to wait until David returned that evening to let him know about the lizard. "You want to take a guess how many lizards die every day in Indonesia of natural causes?" he replied. "It probably had nothing to do with the spray."

"But it's possible that eating the bugs that were killed by the spray was what killed it," she persisted, briefly hopeful that P— might yet forgive her, and restore her own self-image as an enlightened woman, so different from the other expatriate wives.

"It's possible. But unless you know for certain, there's no sense losing sleep over it."

No sense. And she didn't. Eight months later they were in Turkey, all her energies devoted to the rapidly growing Geoff, and attending her new classes. Nor did she think, now, that if David was in the early stages of Alzheimer's, or some other neurological disorder, it was his payment for that long ago injury to the environment. She put no stock in the notion that all causes were connected. The cosmos didn't work that way, the cosmos was random. Beth didn't know who Pol Pot was, or why

moths

the Vietnamese soldiers had imprisoned Dinh. But she knew what didn't need to be taught: that he had done something remarkable when he walked out of Vietnam and through Cambodia and that that achievement, coupled with his ability to tap rubber and build houses represented something you held on to once you met it, something that made it even more delightful when he lifted her up, high over his head. David had done that twice. Once when she told him that she was pregnant with Geoff. The second time when they learned they were being sent to London, their last international posting before coming home. London was where she studied pastel portraiture and where David met his second wife. "You know me too well," he had said, when he explained why he wanted a divorce. Meaning: he wanted to be found novel, to inspire pleasure and surprise. Certainly in Indonesia David could still arouse that sentiment in her. In Turkey, less so, and even less thereafter. And how would her relationship with P— have changed over those years, if they had stayed in Indonesia? Could she have repaired the rift that opened between them?

She turned the coffee maker off, and rinsed out the carafe in the sink before replacing it. Then she turned out the light and climbed the stairs.

She found David on the couch in the living room. He was stretched out, asleep. She hadn't seen him so in a long time, and crept up to stand alongside. She knew he wouldn't approve of her being sentimental. Everyone looked vulnerable when they slept. But there was no doubt that he looked older. The modern conceit was that age didn't have to be a time of diminishing powers. But it was foolish to forget that for many, it would be.

He opened his eyes and smiled. Shifted, to make room for her to sit. Had he forgotten they were divorced? Then, because she'd sometimes wondered what it would be like between them now if they had stayed together, she sat down.

"Do you remember the man who was our gardener, in Indonesia? Well, he was much more than the gardener. But that's how he introduced himself."

The wary look returned. He nodded.

"I've been trying to remember his name, but I can't."

"We had a lot of servants," he said.

"That's true," she murmured.

The first doctor they had seen was young, and kindly. "What kind of work do you do?" he asked, once David had answered all the simple questions: the day, the month, the year, the president.

"I'm in personal finance now. I was in international banking."

"Really? So you worked overseas?"

"Sure."

"What countries?"

David opened his mouth — but then his brow clouded over, and he looked to her.

She wondered if P— was still alive. He'd had children, and must have grandchildren by this time. Even great-grandchildren. Was his wife still alive? Katherine had never met her. Surely he wouldn't still be working for expatriate families, smoothing the way for them so they could return to their countries of origin more or less unchanged?

Pramana — all at once, there was his name; some chemical trace, started hours earlier, when she had first recalled him, now completed. She wished that she could see him again, to ask him what had happened in the meantime, and tell him what was happening to them. Suddenly it seemed he was the only person in the wide world who would understand her loss and offer any solace.

at home anywhere

It was around the time that both his children were in college and his wife went back to school that Douglas took to staying on the train a stop past his station on Friday evenings. This placed him at the eastern end of Atlantic Avenue, where he could visit the Arab-owned grocery stores that lined that portion of the route he would take home later, on foot. Everything about the stores on that stretch of the avenue — smaller and busier, with more transactions taking place in languages other than English — made them seem more "authentic" than the ones at the western end. He liked the way things were displayed: lentils and dried fruits in barrels along the floor and trays of feta cheese inside the refrigerated cases. The swash of Arabic letters on some of the packaged items made it seem he'd traveled much further away from home than a single subway stop. What most appealed to him, however, were the greetings his arrival inspired. "Hello, my friend," the storekeepers said, once they began to identify him as a regular visitor, sometimes the moment he stepped over the threshold. And while he understood that in that context the word *friend* did not denote the intimate relationship his definition described; it warmed him, made him feel as though he had been included in an embrace.

For a time, he limited himself to visiting the food stores, where he'd pick up feta cheese and coffee, or pita bread and dates. A native diffidence kept him out of the stores that sold books and clothing. Most of the volumes displayed in those shop windows were religious in nature, with titles, when they were printed in English, like *Christ in Islam* and *Prayer*, and that made him feel these stores shouldn't be entered lightly. Though he wasn't at all religious, he appreciated the sentiment that led people to consecrate certain places, and tried to be respectful even if he didn't believe.

What took him over the threshold of the first dry goods store was a notion that he might find something for his brother's birthday inside. Back in high school his older brother Eric had been the lead singer in a local band. Onstage Eric often wore the kind of embroidered vest popularized by the rock stars of the time. The vest was made of brown suede, with lamb's fur sticking out at the armholes and neck. Douglas had borrowed it to wear one Halloween and somehow it had been misplaced over the years. He'd been thinking how funny it would be to find one like it, and give it to his brother as a gift.

But there wasn't anything like that vest on sale. Instead he found a few racks of the long garments he'd seen local women wearing, alongside shelves holding head scarves. There were two kinds of scarves: the ones manufactured expressly for the purpose, packaged in clear plastic with portraits of smiling women on the front; and the kind that could be purposed according to the wearer's need, and required pins to keep them fastened around the head. Another rack held the trouser outfits some of the neighborhood men wore. Between the two, books had been set out on a large, flat display case. There was music, a vocalist singing in a style Douglas recognized as devotional in nature from listening to a late-night public radio program. He met the gaze of the man at the counter on his way in, and nodded then, and again as he exited. Both times he received an answering nod, reassuringly disinterested, which made him think he wasn't breaking any taboos by browsing. So the dry goods stores became a regular part of his Friday visit to the avenue.

The store that quickly became his favorite was tended by two teenaged boys and their elderly father. The boys were often chattering to

at home anywhere

each other when he entered. He learned they were from Pakistan during his second visit, when the more outgoing of the pair, noticing Douglas' interest in a wall map of Islam's holy places, pointed out the shrines in that country.

When the father was in, which was the case most of the time, he sat behind a kind of stall at the front of the shop, surrounded by a mass of small items like soap and toothpaste, while the boys stood or sat farther back with the books and clothing. Most of the toiletries were familiar brands, but a close inspection of the labels often revealed an ingredient list printed in Arabic and a company address somewhere in the Middle East. These sat alongside items whose non-religious equivalents were available everywhere: oversized key chains, here printed with the declaration "I Love Allah," and wall plaques featuring prayers and images of Mecca. A few of the objects were completely novel, and among these was the bouquet of twigs that sat in a canister alongside the cash register. Once, when the father was out and one of the boys had taken his place at the stall, Douglas asked what they were.

"These are the Prophet's toothbrush," the boy readily replied.

"Do they work?" Douglas inquired.

"Very well, yes," the boy said, eagerly; "If you try, you will like it very much, *insha-Allah.*" He offered Douglas one for free, but Douglas declined. The reference to Mohammed gave the twigs a religious significance that triggered his natural reserve. And he didn't want to take advantage of the boy's good nature.

"No problem, my friend," the young man said, smiling as he replaced the twig inside the canister. They were charming boys. Douglas thought they must attend some kind of religious school that required limited attendance, if they attended school at all, and then spent the rest of the day in the store. They seemed happy enough. Their father must certainly enjoy having them around so much. Of course his own children would have hated such a life. But that was the world, wasn't it? How dull it would be otherwise.

The first item he bought from the boys and their father was a bar of soap. At home afterwards he unpacked and put away the groceries he'd purchased in the other stores along the avenue before removing the soap from its sack. Sharon entered as he inspected the label.

"What's that?" she asked, with mild curiosity.

at home anywhere

"It's soap. I got it at one of the stores on Atlantic. Two boys run it with their father. They're young — teenagers. Very friendly. I just couldn't walk out without buying something."

She came to his side and peered at the soap. "It's Palmolive," she said, quizzically.

"But look at the writing — see? It's Arabic."

"Right. But it's Palmolive. I can get that at Key Food." His face fell, and she added, affectionately: "You're funny. Anyway, I'm going to order out. What do you want?"

"Oh — anything," he replied, disguising his irritation as he left the room. "Surprise me."

Upstairs, at his dresser, he wondered at his response to Sharon's gentle teasing. Why had he felt so wronged? He agreed, it was foolish to buy a product that he didn't really need, that was manufactured by a corporate giant, just because the label bore a little foreign lettering.

Turning the soap over in his hand, he read the place of manufacture: Lahore. Deep down he knew the source of his distress. He'd never go to Lahore. Even if he went now, he'd only be a tourist, and he'd meant to *live* somewhere else. Before meeting Sharon at college, his plan was to enter the Peace Corps after getting his degree. In the early phase of their courtship she expressed the same desire, and he took her at her word. She was a French major, after all, and he knew there were Peace Corps volunteers in Francophone Africa. He even remembered stifling pangs of guilty jealousy at the thought that her language skills might make her more valuable to the Corps than he was. His concern was premature. In time he discovered that many of her enthusiasms reflected only superficial interest. But by then he was in love, and couldn't hold the habit against her.

In their final year, Sharon and her best girlfriends decided to follow graduation with a summer of touring around Europe before entering the job market. Douglas didn't have any plans beyond working at the summer camp he'd attended as a child. So on graduation day he asked Sharon to marry him. He couldn't think of any other way to ensure that they would be together again in the fall.

In September she got a job offer at a public middle school on the East Side. She said it was a place people waited years to get into and that it would be crazy to turn it down. They got married that spring, by which time she identified so completely with the mission of the school that

at home anywhere

there was no question of going to Francophone Africa or anywhere else. After a couple of false starts in Wall Street training programs, Douglas found a niche putting out promotional materials for a bank. Then Aiden came along, and they decided not to wait too long to have Paige so that the children would keep each other company. The idea of going into the Peace Corps rapidly became a kind of inside joke, shorthand for youthful naïveté. Sharon never expressed any regrets, but he felt like he'd given something up — oh, voluntarily; he loved his kids and Sharon, and given the opportunity to do everything over again, he supposed his life wouldn't have unfolded that differently. Only her amusement at his delight in the soap label suggested that she'd forgotten his sacrifice or never appreciated that he'd made one. Like most people, at heart she imagined that everyone was really like her and wanted what she did. But if now he wanted to engage in a little exploration, even if his travels only took him as far as a store on Atlantic Avenue, he didn't want that instinct mocked.

He decided that he wouldn't show Sharon any of his future purchases. Or tell her any more about the boys and their father. He might change his mind, but for now he meant to withhold the details of his deepening acquaintance.

He felt better, once that decision was made, and dropped the soap into his sock drawer. To be forgotten, as most souvenirs were.

No one who knew Douglas as a child would have been surprised at the pleasure he took in his shopping ventures. His interest in other cultures began when he was nine, and overheard a neighbor tell his mother that a Christian group had purchased the two-family home at the corner of their block for the purpose of housing missionaries for brief stays before they were posted overseas. Thereafter he found excuses to play at that end of the street, waiting for the visitors to appear. They were usually family people, and he would hang around tossing a ball or riding his bike in circles until the children came outside, and then introduce himself with the offer of a ride or a turn with the ball. The missionaries were frequently Americans from the south and west, whose dress and speech varied enough from his own to make the wait worthwhile. Once in a while a Korean or Indian family arrived, on a return trip from a bible study program somewhere in the American interior, and that was even

at home anywhere

better. He quickly took up his new friends' customs — leaving his shoes outside the door when he was invited inside to play, for example. He could tell their parents appreciated the gesture, as the invitation was often expanded to include their evening meal. After the families moved on, Douglas liked to try out the practices he'd observed in his own home: taking off his shoes before coming inside, or placing a bowl of water near his plate to wash his hands during a meal. He remembered how much his mother seemed to enjoy those little borrowings. "You'd be at home anywhere," she said, pleased and surprised at his mimicry as he sat cross-legged on the floor to eat his lunch because he'd seen a Japanese family do so in a filmstrip at school; as though the one characteristic she'd never expected a child of hers to express was an interest in foreigners.

Domestic goods continued to comprise the class of articles that Douglas traded in during the first few months of his acquaintance with the family in the dry goods store: toothpaste, combs, pocket mirrors, small packets of Kleenex. Then one day a book caught his eye, entitled *Muslim Heroes of the Crusades*. Glancing through the pages, he recognized a name: Saladin.

"You are liking history," one of the brothers said, joining him as he started towards the cash register with the book.

"That was my college major," Douglas replied, a little sheepishly.

"This is very, very good book," the boy answered, "very interesting."

The book was short, only 120 pages, and he read it that evening. He was relieved when the boys didn't ask about it the next time he visited the store. He supposed that was because he already knew what a misadventure the crusades had been, and how much more tolerant Saladin was than his Christian counterparts. The campaigns the Europeans fought were hardly the glorious struggle the early church advertised, and the book's brief account confirmed Douglas's understanding. Still, he guessed the topic might prove a little tricky to navigate with people from that part of the world. He preferred to keep things pleasant and positive, and was glad to find the boys just the same as always the next time he saw them.

at home anywhere

One evening late in May, Douglas purchased a head scarf. No doubt the quality of the day inspired him; it was the kind that made him swear he could feel the sap rising in the city's trees, calling up some analogous substance in him. He couldn't say his action was entirely spontaneous, however. A mild curiosity about how the scarves were constructed had been growing in him for some time — whenever he saw a pretty women wearing one, in fact. Until then, he'd always managed to subdue the occasional impulse to examine one more closely, out of concern for the sensibilities of the local storekeepers, who might not like the idea of a non-believer pawing over something meant to symbolize an observant woman's honor. But by this time he felt so comfortable in the company of the boys and their father, that on his way around the book table, passing the shelf full of the scarves in their plastic bags, he simply picked one up — a peach-colored one — and, without breaking stride, presented it at the counter to pay. The father was at the register on this occasion. He looked at the package, then at Douglas. "This is for children," he said. "You want for children?"

Douglas struggled to disguise his sudden discomfiture. Should he make something up about whom the scarf was intended for? A wrong word now might invite the man's censure, and he would have to give up his weekly visits. His mind moved quickly through the possibilities for composing an excuse. He could simply say he'd changed his mind and leave. Hope they forgot his lapse in etiquette by his next visit. Or it might be better to complete the transaction — if he didn't act suspiciously, perhaps they wouldn't view him that way.

Somehow he managed to meet the man's gaze and answer calmly. "Oh, is it? No, I want it for an adult," he replied, thinking if he showed the scarf to Sharon, that would be true. The man summoned one of his sons from the rear of the store. After an exchange in their own language, the boy motioned for Douglas to return to where the scarves were displayed. Then he fanned through the packages so Douglas could choose, which he did by nodding at another peach-colored one. Once the selection was made, the boy carried it to the front of the store and placed it inside a shopping bag while his father rang up the sale. Neither one registered surprise or disapproval.

Douglas thought he'd succeeded in hiding his unease from the old man, but that uncertainty, and his own recklessness, nagged at him as he

at home anywhere

made his way along the avenue. What had possessed him to forget his usual caution? After all, he owned no other religious tokens. No crosses, or ankhs, or even astrological symbols because he didn't think they should be used as casual decoration. Nor did Sharon. He had thought his initial impulse arose from simple curiosity, but now he wondered if he wanted to see her in the scarf? He passed a dozen Muslim women on the way home, some in ordinary printed scarves that any woman might wear, only pinned in such a way that their hair was completely covered. Others wore the type he had just purchased. Always before he had privately admired the women without any sense of trespass — just as he admired the pretty women from all the other nations of the world that lived in the city — but today he averted his gaze.

His agitation propelled him up the stairs to his bedroom to hide his purchase before Sharon arrived. Standing in front of his bureau he was surprised to discover that one of the tooth cleaning sticks had been thrown into the bag along with the headscarf. He smiled at the kindness. And was reassured: apparently he hadn't caused offense.

He heard Sharon enter the house, and hurriedly shoved the stick and the scarf under his dress shirts where they joined a growing trove of items purchased on his Friday walks: nail clippers, credit card holders, shaving cream, multiple bars of soap. He'd always taken care of his own shirts, bringing them to the laundry and picking them up again. So the drawer was a good place to hide his treasures; Sharon never went near it.

Entering the kitchen to ask his wife about her day, he was startled by how undressed she seemed with her head bare. He had to glance away, and then force his gaze back to meet hers, as she expected him to. The sensation didn't last; within seconds she looked perfectly ordinary again, and he chalked up her sudden strangeness to a kind of tourist's lag.

Sharon had brought home a bottle of wine and now busied herself opening it, and heating up leftovers for dinner. They drank almost the entire bottle, with most of it swirling inside his stomach by the end of their meal. While they ate she told him a long story about one of her students and what a sad home life he had, but Douglas was only half listening. He was thinking about the storekeeper and his sons, trying to imagine their domestic life. The boys were so much younger than their father — was their mother much younger also? As Sharon rose to take some of the dishes away, he envisioned the boys embracing their parents

at home anywhere

before going off to bed, and then their father uncovering his wife's head and stroking her hair. He stood up, wanting to continue the communion he felt with the man, and crossed to where Sharon was standing at the sink with her back to him. He wrapped his arms around her, and kissed the nape of her neck, but she didn't return the embrace. "School night," she warned. One of her classes was being conducted online. She had to log in for a specified block of time each week.

    He retreated to the living room to watch the news. It wasn't until he was in bed, listening to the click of the keyboard in the next room, that he thought of the scarf again. What would she say if he asked her to try it on? He remembered the sense he'd had, at seeing her for the first time since the morning, that there was something amiss in her appearance. How would she react to that admission? Would she take him seriously? Or scoff at the notion that his perceptions could be that easily influenced? An hour on the street where some of the women wore head-scarves and a rare few were veiled and suddenly it seemed to him that everyone should be?

    It might be better to present the scarf to her as a sort of joke-gift — the equivalent of the "French maid" outfit a neighbor had worn one Halloween. He'd been on trick-or-treat duty that evening, taking the kids around the neighborhood. When the woman opened the door he was stunned, momentarily unable to reply to her faux-French query as to his candy preferences. Periodically, as he moved from house to house along the street with Aiden and Paige, he'd glanced back to see her greeting new rounds of children in her black miniskirt and tiny white apron and hat. Of her husband he thought, *lucky bastard*.

    Later, he'd mentioned the costume to Sharon, half-seriously suggesting that she get one for the next Halloween. As he had expected, she greeted the proposal with derision. "Yeah, right," she scoffed. If she'd been less contemptuous he might have tried to explain that of course he didn't want her to be a maid, only pretend. Did that mean something sinister? Their neighbor hadn't seemed sinister in her costume. Sharon's response in that case left little doubt as to what her reaction would be to a request to try on the scarf. The prospect of costuming herself as an observant Muslim woman would have no more appeal than acting out his French maid fantasy. She'd scorn the idea, and him for making the request.

at home anywhere

Nevertheless, it became a kind of game he played thereafter, to mentally furnish all the women he found appealing, at work or on the block, in colored scarves, and to picture Sharon in one. Later he added another conceit: that they owned the store on Atlantic Avenue, and that the boys from the store were their sons. His own children had no part in these imaginings. That didn't trouble him — these were private fictions, after all.

The kids returned only briefly that summer. The family was reunited for all of about a week, near the end of August. Douglas wanted to spend as much time as possible with his children before they had to leave again, so he dropped the excursions to Atlantic Avenue from his schedule temporarily, although the family did eat out at their favorite Lebanese restaurant just before the two flew back to school. Right after that his department undertook a long-anticipated move from the financial district in lower Manhattan to offices in a new complex in Brooklyn, and for a time he was there so late every day, and even during the weekend following the move, that right into early September most of his usual activities had to be put off.

The transfer from Manhattan meant that his office wasn't directly affected by the events of the morning of 9/11. Though, as the day wore on, and the seriousness of the situation became apparent, everyone was involved, in one way or another. Sharon was the first to alert him to what was happening — a teacher at her school with a free first period had the radio on in her room, and had called her friends to let them know. Douglas turned his radio on after hanging up with her. Once he overcame his initial skepticism that what she had described could actually be taking place, he called anyone who wasn't already in the office to tell them to stay home if they hadn't left yet, or turn back if they were en route. At mid-morning his remaining staff went to the Brooklyn Bridge to hand out water to the people crossing over on foot; he didn't see them again that day. Sharon called at least a dozen times to compare notes about what was happening in their respective locations, and to let him to know that she had gotten through to the kids, and finally to tell him that she was going to stay with friends who lived uptown that night. He remained

at home anywhere

in his office, glued to the radio and to the window, where he watched throngs of people passing through the streets, dust-covered and subdued, until it started to get dark. Then he set out for home, remembering other times the city had taken to its feet like this: a blackout, a transit strike. But it had never been this quiet. The eerie quiet of self-imposed silence in the wake of something awful, that everyone sensed would not soon be over.

A number of racially-motivated incidents occurred around the country in the weeks following the attacks. In one case a Sikh man was murdered, his attackers mistaking his turban for a symbol of Muslim faith. The question of Saudi complicity arose since many of the attackers had been nationals of that country. Reports appeared that the Saudi government exported a particular form of fundamentalist Islam to other nations around the world, though that government denied the charges. Through it all, the president urged Americans to remain peaceful and not to judge all the followers of Islam by the violent actions of a few. A new domestic security agency was formed. One of the new department's first acts was to ask Muslim men to voluntarily present themselves for questioning. There was a lot of discussion in the papers and on the commentary shows about whether civil liberties were taking a back seat to security, but most Americans seemed willing to make the trade-off, and Douglas found himself in cautious agreement with the general feeling that some lapses in surveillance had occurred, and had to be made up for.

Mosques known for fundamentalist preaching were subject to the new surveillance measures, and one Saturday morning a few weeks after the attack the local newspaper ran a photograph of a mosque on Atlantic Avenue, identifying it as one of the sites under review. Douglas recognized the mosque: it stood alongside the store the two boys ran with their father.
Sharon entered the kitchen. "I'm making coffee. Want some?"
"No thanks."
She was at the sink, filling the pot when Douglas added, half seriously, "I guess this means I'd better get rid of my soap."
"What?" She had plugged in the coffee machine, and now, as he'd hoped, came to stand at his side, peering over his shoulder at the photograph.

at home anywhere

He explained, "Remember that soap I bought on Atlantic Avenue? I showed it to you. It had the Arabic writing on it. The store where I bought it is right next to this mosque."

She bent closer to read the caption under the photograph. "Well," she said, straightening, "I don't think you need to worry about a bar of soap." Then, after a pause, added: "I think I might not go shopping there for a while, though." He did not imagine the contrast in tone between the two statements: the first made lightly; the second soberly. "I haven't," he replied. He pictured the boys and their father standing just outside the frame of the picture. He missed them.

He hadn't seen them since late August. For the first week following the attack, Douglas found that he wanted to return directly home after work, to watch all the news broadcasts about the aftermath. As time went on his reasons for staying away from the stores on Atlantic Avenue grew more complex. It was in the papers that some of the Muslim charities operating in the United States had links to militant Muslim groups overseas. He'd often deposited the loose change he got from his purchases into the collecting cans many of the shops along Atlantic Avenue kept atop their counters, and was uncertain how to inquire of the owners where their sympathies lay. Had he inadvertently funded violence anywhere? Paid for explosives rather than for the care and feeding of the children featured on the cans? There were still people who charged the government with relying too heavily on circumstantial evidence to paint people as terrorist sympathizers. Whether or not that was true, Douglas decided that he didn't want to test his luck.

Of course he had only mentioned the soap to Sharon as a sort of stand-in for the scarf that lay buried under the shirts inside his bureau. That was his most compromising souvenir. If he had shown it to her before, she might have teased him about it, but that would have made the purchase seem ordinary. In both their minds the scarf would be placed in the same class as all the other tokens he'd bought, an armchair traveler's collectibles. Now she might find the fact that he'd hidden the scarf so long unsettling, even creepy. *I should get rid of it,* he thought.

Then he thought: *how ridiculous!* All the terror talk was getting to him. It was only a memento, after all. He had a right to keep it!

He glanced back at the newspaper. The caption under the photograph reminded him that a plot to bomb the subway had been hatched in an

at home anywhere

apartment building near the mosque a few years earlier. One of the actors in that incident attended the mosque. Douglas remembered the helicopter that hovered all day over the junction of Atlantic and Pacific Streets after the bomb-makers' roommate tipped off the police. At that point it struck him that the store might have been under surveillance *before* 9/11. His visits to the shop and his friendly relations with the owner and his sons might already have been observed.

That thought amplified his conviction that the scarf should be discarded. He would need to disguise it before getting rid of it to prevent Sharon or his neighbors from seeing it in the trash.

Sharon sat down with her coffee as he set aside the paper.

"Are you finished with that?" she asked.

"Yep," he said, passing it across the table as he rose. Climbing the stairs to the bedroom he decided to bring the scarf to work in his briefcase. He could put it in an envelope here, and then into the trash in one of the office restrooms; that would make the disposal completely anonymous.

But at the sight of the peach scarf sitting at the bottom of his drawer, underneath three levels of his shirts, he hesitated. It was only an artifact, after all — historical evidence of his curiosity, if nothing else. Artifacts shouldn't be destroyed just because what they represented became controversial. The chances of its being discovered were very, very small. Why shouldn't he just leave it where it was?

Then he thought, *what if New York was attacked again?* And at some point his children had to go through his things? What would they make of finding a Muslim headscarf hidden underneath his dress shirts? They might infer that he had harbored some exotic fantasy about veiled women, and that would embarrass them and make him seem pathetic. He really should have revealed the scarf to Sharon earlier, presented it as a completely ordinary ethnic token; the contemporary equivalent of the suede vest his brother had worn for his performances with the rock band. But he hadn't, and now his interest would be much harder to explain.

Quickly, before his resolve weakened, he found a manila envelope atop his desk and slipped in the scarf, still in its wrapper. Then he got his briefcase and placed the envelope inside. Finally he set the briefcase deep under his desk to make sure nothing called it to Sharon's attention until he could carry it to work on Monday morning. Once that was done he felt an enormous sense of relief, as he had years earlier when he made his first marijuana buy without getting caught. He felt certain he would not be discovered.

The mosque wasn't mentioned in the newspaper again. For a short time, the appearance of any woman in a head scarf unsettled him, reminding him of his conflicted attachment to the one he'd discarded. Very soon, however, it was as if someone else had purchased the scarf, and hidden it, and thrown it away.

Now that he worked in Brooklyn, Douglas could walk home from work and usually did. But one Friday afternoon in April, returning early from a meeting in Manhattan, he dozed, and stayed on the train until it reached Atlantic Avenue. Noticing his error, he cursed under his breath. He was still troubled by a sense of guilt for placing money in the charity cans in the shops upstairs, and had no wish to resurrect that emotion by going past his old haunts. To avoid the prospect, he would have to use the stairs and cross over to the other platform to wait for a train that would take him a stop in the opposite direction. Inwardly berating himself for his lapse, he made the switch, and once on the other side of the station sat down on a bench and pulled a newspaper out of his briefcase. But he couldn't distract himself, and when after fifteen minutes the train had still not arrived, he decided to walk home after all.

As he climbed the steps out of the station, he thought of the elderly shopkeeper and his sons. By that time it had been many months since he'd last seen them, though he thought of them whenever news appeared about the sweeps of immigrant men being conducted in communities with large numbers of Middle Eastern inhabitants. Some of the men caught up in the sweeps were deported for visa violations. In some cases their families were left behind. Had the shopkeeper and his sons been swept up? Was their store still open? Had they been sent back?

He decided he would glance into the store as he walked past, to see if they were still there. But he wouldn't go in.

To his dismay, however, one of the boys was standing in the entrance and recognized Douglas before he could avoid being seen. "My friend!" the boy cried out, and waved.

He couldn't ignore the greeting. With a measured step, so that anyone observing would notice his reluctance, he walked toward the

at home anywhere

boy, who held out his hand as the distance between them shortened, pumping eagerly when Douglas brought up his own.

"We don't see you for a *long* time!"

"Well, my company moved. So it's been very busy at work. And then, with everything that's happening…" Douglas shrugged and shook his head to indicate his inadequacy to the task of explaining the mix of considerations that had kept him away.

"Come in, please, my friend; my brother is here and my father also," the boy said, either ignoring or misunderstanding the reference, gesturing for Douglas to follow him. And, unhappily, Douglas followed, because it would have seemed rude not to.

As usual, the father was seated behind the counter just inside the entrance. His expression revealed surprise and some alarm at seeing Douglas, but before he could speak his son addressed him rapidly, in high excitement, in their own language. He nodded towards Douglas, soberly, and then seemed to answer the boy, whose speech had apparently contained a question that the old man was now attempting to answer—negatively, to judge by his son's obvious disappointment. Meanwhile, his brother had come forward from the rear of the store, and after greeting Douglas, he too seemed to try to convince his father of something. At the end of his speech the old man looked at Douglas as though weighing their arguments. Finally he spoke. "My friend," he said, "my sons want to know if you will help us."

At first, Douglas thought anxiety must have caused him to misapprehend the man's words, which, as he heard them, represented the worst possible outcome of his decision to abandon his plan to walk past the store without going in. But when the three kept looking at him, expectantly, he realized that he hadn't misheard; they wanted something from him. His first impulse was to flee. He never had to see these people again; no one would ever know that he hadn't heard them out.

But that impulse quickly died. As he was being drawn into the shop, the old sensation of being happily out of his usual element fell over him. The father's sudden, direct appeal gave him no time to rehearse a negative response, and as the seconds ticked past he found that he didn't want to. Nodding, he replied, "Sure. What's the problem?"

One of the boys gestured for his father to retrieve something from behind the counter. A manila envelope: large, padded, overstuffed.

49

at home anywhere

Taking it from the old man's hand, he brought it toward Douglas, who glanced obliquely at the address and then away. Someplace on Coney Island Avenue.

"We want to mail these things, but government is everywhere, watching us. We don't have papers. We can't go anywhere or they will send us away. Please, can you do this for us?"

"What's in it?" Douglas asked, straining to sound merely curious.

"Letters from families in Pakistan. Their men are here. They know us. Sometimes the men, they need to move, they change address, but we can find them. But now we are afraid, if we try to mail these letters, they will be opened. And these are..." He halted, seeming to search for a word. "...*personal* letters. You have family, my friend?"

Douglas nodded, playing for time. He gazed again at the envelope, purposely avoiding the address in case anyone, afterwards, asked: *could he remember where it was going?* "Yes," he said, remembering his fantasy of running the store with Sharon, of having these sons; "I have family."

Then he thought, *Who knows what the envelope really contains?* And why did they consider a trip to the post office more dangerous than any other excursion they might make? Surely if the immigration service knew their status, they wouldn't hesitate to find them inside their store? The boys stared at him with expressions of pure entreaty, so he turned to the old man, who seemed miles away, regarding his sons with melancholy devotion — certain they would be disappointed; powerless to prevent that outcome. Then Douglas heard himself say, "No problem. I'll mail it for you."

The boys were effusively grateful, stating repeatedly that God would bless him. Briefly, Douglas was filled with elation. There was hope; the world could be changed, people would trust each other again. Then he remembered the newspaper story about the mosque next door and his anxiety returned. "How quickly do you want it to get there? Can it go by regular mail or do you want it to go express...?" he asked, attempting, by focusing on the details of the transaction, to suppress his rising apprehension.

"How you think is better, my friend, you decide."

"Does it have to go out today?"

"Please, yes, it is here too long, the men are waiting."

at home anywhere

He glanced at the clock behind the register. It wasn't yet five. Still time to make it to the branch a few blocks away. Or would it be better to go to the main post office downtown? More anonymous? No, whatever got the envelope out of his hands most quickly was best.

"Well, in that case, I'll take it to the post office right here on Atlantic," he said. "I'm pretty sure I can get it there before they close."

The old man opened the cash register and looked at him expectantly.

"No, no, that's not necessary; I'll handle it, I'm sure it's not going to cost that much," Douglas protested. Certainly he didn't want to be seen taking money from them!

"Next time, you tell me the cost," the man said, "I will pay."

"Sure, we'll see..."

"Thank you, my friend."

"No problem. Well..." Douglas dropped his gaze to the items arranged for sale below the cash register and quickly chose a bar of soap. He needed the bag he would get with the purchase. He would carry the envelope in that. He had the vague notion he would be safer that way: if anyone approached who seemed to know what he was carrying, he could drop the bag quickly and get away.

The old man wouldn't accept money for the soap, however, so Douglas stuffed the one dollar bill he'd intended to use for that purpose into a trouser pocket and left the store in a kind of daze.

The plastic bag, with the soap and the envelope inside, dangled from the end of his left arm, which felt so outsized and ungainly that he was certain all eyes must be drawn to it. As he walked he averted his gaze, avoiding the faces of the people passing by. Some of them might really be government agents — that much was plausible; in fact it was likely there were undercover people posted nearby to observe the mosque. They might have seen him take the envelope and would, any second now, close in around him and demand to know what he was doing. At every intersection, when he had to stop, he fought the impulse to take the envelope out for examination. In the brief time he'd handled it, it had seemed to hold paper, densely packed. He had no doubt that it really did contain the letters the boys had said were inside, not instructions for making a dirty bomb or anthrax powder. He would not believe those boys, so lively and devoted to their father, were capable of that kind of violence. But he might be watched, followed.

at home anywhere

The state of heightened alert, of barely stifled panic, stayed with him as he walked toward the post office, and while he waited in line, and became almost unbearable when he passed the envelope across the counter to the clerk, who seemed to frown at the address. He waited to be asked to step to another window to see a supervisor. Or for a voice from behind him to say: "Please come this way." But apparently the clerk's concern was for the envelope's mail-worthiness, and not its destination. With an air of satisfaction in handling the repair, she added tape to the corners, and then tossed it onto a scale. "How you want this to go?" she asked. "First class," he croaked. Seconds later he'd paid, and was retreating from the window. He had spied a wastebasket on the way in; just before exiting, he dropped in the plastic bag, weighted by the bar of soap.

Outside again Douglas set off, facing away from the large, brick building he'd just left. Instinctively he hunched his shoulders, as though half-expecting the building to blow up behind him. Then he pictured the two boys and their father. No, of course not.

At first he walked with no destination in mind, glancing down twice within his first thirty steps to rid himself of the sudden compulsion that the envelope was still somewhere on his person. Except for his first glance, when the boy had shown him the envelope in the store, he'd avoided reading the complete address. But just before the postal clerk had completed her choreography of taping and stamping, he'd tried to commit it to memory. Now, hastily, he pulled out a pen and wrote it down on the bill he'd stuffed into his pocket earlier. The first line of the address contained the name of a mosque.

He shoved the money back into his pocket and set off again, but a few feet further on his steps faltered. He couldn't go home yet. He had to see the mosque, to reassure himself that it was real.

And if the mosque wasn't there?

He pushed the thought aside.

After a short train ride, he hurried along the streets between the station and the traffic circle at the corner of the park. The bus he needed was already waiting — Douglas remembered that was the end of the line, and the bus would stand there a while. He jogged towards it anyway,

at home anywhere

eager to find the mosque and put the events of the afternoon behind him. He paid his fare and chose a seat alongside a window so he could read the street signs. When half a dozen other riders had found places, the bus started off, picking up speed as it ran downhill alongside the park until it crossed the juncture with Ocean Parkway. It slowed down on Coney Island Avenue, which Douglas knew as one of the great arteries that led into the interior of the borough, though he rarely had cause to visit the neighborhoods there. For a long stretch, the streets were deserted and the buildings shabby. Here and there awnings lettered with the names of various kinds of small businesses hung over darkened windows. Then suddenly that changed, and there were people everywhere, most wearing saris and tunics underneath western-style sweaters and coats, streaming in and out of shops, past boxes of vegetables stacked alongside cartons of bargain toilet paper and generic dishwashing liquid. He saw the mosque in passing and called out: "Stop!"

The bus carried him two blocks past his destination, and he walked back hastily, desperate to complete his task and go home. A handful of men stood outside the mosque, which occupied a building that had been awkwardly converted from some other use and painted bright blue. They regarded him suspiciously as he approached, and moved together when it became apparent that he meant to cross directly in front of them. He nodded, and one or two nodded tensely in return. Their faces cleared when they saw that he did not intend to stop.

After that he was so relieved at finding what he'd been looking for that he didn't immediately notice the effect he was having on other bystanders. Once past the mosque he kept his gaze trained on the ground. All manner of shoe and sandal met his glance: none fine, all worn; feet spilling out of some of them, not filling others adequately so they clattered on the street. What a joke he was, what an amateur. As though he could really have gotten close to those boys and their father, as though Sharon would agree to wear the scarf, as though they could go visiting them, like a couple in Lahore. Disgusted with himself he glanced up and caught the hard stare of a man inside a newspaper store. A few steps further on, whispered comments among a trio at the door of a restaurant. They think I'm FBI, he realized with dismay. After going out of his way to help those boys and their father!

Then he thought, it didn't matter what they thought of him. He

at home anywhere

wouldn't be coming here again.

Or should he persist in the acquaintance? What if he returned to the boys and their father to let them know their package had been safely mailed? They might ask him to do something else. Mail another package, or undertake some other errand.

He imagined the scene. The old man bringing forward the envelope. The boys looking on to see what he would do. And even now, he couldn't say that he would question them any more closely before accepting their charge. How could that be, after everything that had happened? Oh, but that was easy — he didn't want to know that people weren't as he'd always believed: a collection of tribes whose superficial differences disguised an underlying store of mutual good will.

Just before boarding the bus, he bought a bottle of water from a corner newsstand. He wasn't thirsty. He wanted to pass along the dollar bill that contained the mosque's address.

On the bus he collapsed into a double seat, laying his briefcase flat on its side so no one would join him. He stared out the window as his journey flew past in reverse: the bleak avenue giving way to the uphill run alongside the park, the empty shops replaced by rows of houses.

"You'd be at home anywhere." He remembered how pleased he'd been to earn his mother's recognition of...what?

The pleasure he took in entertaining the possibility of living a life unlike his own.

An empty boast, when now there was nowhere he wanted to go.

Felix and adauctus

Paul had been sharing Sonia's home for five months, but still entered cautiously. His dog, a shepherd named Luke, rushed forward when he let himself in on the ground floor, followed by Sonia's golden retriever Finn. Mischa, her elderly elkhound, remained on his rug under the grand piano, but lifted his head. As Paul knelt to greet the dogs his eyes adjusted to the gloom, taking in the signs of Sonia's return: the matched set of suitcases in a neat pile at the bottom of the stairs, the water bottle on the coffee table alongside the velvet couch. He listened, but the house seemed empty. He felt grateful for even a short period of time to re-acclimate to her presence. Sonia traveled frequently on the healing circuit, and didn't always let him know in advance when she would return. It never took him long to get used to living there alone.

He passed on to the kitchen to put the groceries away, taking the empty bottle along for disposal, then walked Mischa, as the elkhound could only make it once around the block. Once that was done, he harnessed the other dogs and set off for Prospect Park.

at home anywhere

Paul returned to find Sonia seated on the couch, smoke from an incense stick reflecting the light from the television set. She smiled but remained seated, waiting until he had unharnessed the dogs before speaking.

"Hello, Paul. Back from the park?"

The dogs had already reached her. Finn licked her face and Luke trotted over to Mischa, who managed a feeble bark from his place beneath the piano.

"Yes, it was wonderful. I didn't see any rangers so I let them off the leash." Paul spoke quickly, a little nervous in her presence.

"They look great," she murmured, appreciatively rubbing Finn's neck.

Sonia Fisher was a small woman, just beginning to thicken, with neatly cut shoulder-length silver hair. She dressed usually in dark colors and today was no exception: black cotton tunic over black knit pants, accessorized with a quantity of silver jewelry, some of Native American design, obviously authentic.

"Are you busy right now?"

"Well, I have to go to Mass but I don't have to leave for half an hour."

"Good," she said, shutting off the set. "There's something I'd like to discuss. Shall we sit in here, or move to the dining room where we can see the garden?"

"This is fine, but I need to get something to eat. I worked at the co-op today before shopping and I haven't eaten anything in hours."

"Oh, please, get something first!"

"Would you like anything?"

"No thanks," she said, but then, as he entered the kitchen, she changed her mind. "On second thought, I think I left some wine in the refrigerator before I went away. Would you mind pouring me a glass?"

Paul winced. He had purchased a replacement bottle, but it wasn't chilled. "I'm sorry," he said, returning to the living room to confess, "I finished that the night before last with some pizza I brought in. I have another bottle though. It's in my room. Would you like me to get it?"

As his room was in the basement, he wasn't surprised when she declined.

"No thanks. I'm fine. Just get something for yourself."

Felix and adauctus

"Have you tried this?" he asked, placing the tray between them a few minutes later. "It's a new brand of rice milk. It's really delicious. It's light, but it's still substantial. I brought an extra glass for you if you'd like to try some."

"Oh, I've had soy milk," she replied, dismissively. He must have looked disappointed and, perhaps sensing the potential for injury the refusal contained, she relented: "Oh, did you say *rice* milk? I'm sorry, I'm still a little travel-lagged. Maybe I will try some." He was pleased when she finished the glass. "Thank you," she said, graciously, "That really is very good."

After that she got right to the business at hand: "Did you happen to meet the dog walker you talked about, the one who's in construction?"

"Not today, but I did speak to him last Sunday. Unfortunately he said he's too busy at the moment to take on any new jobs," Paul stoically reported, but his spirits sank at the question. Before leaving on this latest trip, Sonia had taken stock of the house and decided it needed some repairs that Paul obviously wasn't up to. No insult intended, she was careful to reassure him. He was wonderful with the dogs and the vacuuming. But the fire escape on the rear of the building was sagging and flaking: it needed shoring up, scraping and painting. Beneath the vines that covered the front of the house, the brownstone facade, a layer of colored concrete and not really "stone" at all, had begun to deteriorate. And all the windows needed work. Despite her reassurances, Paul grew alarmed at the prospect of having someone else around the place. Sonia exchanged her counseling services for the work her accountant did on her taxes. She did the same thing at the local salon where she had her hair cut. It wasn't implausible that whoever she found to do the big jobs on the house would be open to an arrangement that combined that work with the tasks Paul currently handled, in return for a cheap rent. Sonia might discover that she didn't need two helpers, and Paul would have to look for another place to live.

Sonia sighed. "I'm not surprised. There seems to be remodeling going on all over the neighborhood. There's a dumpster on every block."

"Actually, I did meet someone today who seemed like he might be helpful...," Paul offered, with more assurance than he felt.

"Oh?" Sonia replied, expectantly.

He felt in his pocket for the flyer he'd been handed at the food co-op

at home anywhere

earlier that day, and passed it across to her. "Yes, there's someone at the co-op who does this kind of work," he said, shuddering inwardly at his deception. His introduction made it sound like the stranger who gave him the flyer was a regular patron, someone with whom he was well acquainted. In fact Paul had never seen the man before that day.

Sonia sat forward in her chair to read. "Oh! And he's looking for a place to stay. I've been thinking about letting someone have that room at the front of the house."

"Emma's room?"

Emma was Sonia's youngest daughter. She had graduated college a year earlier and settled in Oregon with her boyfriend. Paul had planned to let another month or two pass before bidding to move into the vacant room himself. He'd had no idea that Sonia had already considered the prospect.

"Yes. It seems a shame to let it sit empty when there's such a need. So, should I call him?"

"It can't hurt to speak to him," Paul replied, suppressing a growing regret that he had mentioned the man.

"What's his name?"

Paul drew a blank. "Isn't it on there?" he asked, frowning, playing for time.

"No. There's a number, but no name."

"It's Tyler," Paul said, memory flooding back. "Tyler Landry."

"I'll call him right now," said Sonia, cheerfully rising and passing into the kitchen, where a telephone hung on the wall. She believed that wireless devices caused brain cancer, and wouldn't have them in the house. But she had equipped her landlines with long enough wires to take a phone nearly anywhere, and Paul waited until she was in the garden before carrying the tray of empty glasses to the sink. Catching his own image in the shiny black door as he approached the refrigerator he reproached himself. Sonia was right; with housing so scarce Emma's room shouldn't go to waste. He had found refuge here. Who was he to play gatekeeper? Recalling Tyler Landry's unhappy expression he thought: *another lamb for Christ.*

Before coming to live with Sonia, Paul had shared a floor-through apartment with a couple for almost a year. Then the woman discovered

Felix and adauctus

that her boyfriend was cheating on her. As Paul was gay, a retaliatory relationship was out of the question, so she moved out. In her absence the boyfriend, who'd previously seemed perfectly comfortable with Paul's orientation, became distant and ill-at-ease. Feeling unwelcome, Paul started looking for another place to live.

He'd found his current living situation through a notice posted on the bulletin board at the Park Slope Food Cooperative. These days, his housing needs met, he enjoyed perusing the board's contents for a quick guide to neighborhood trends. Arriving at the co-op for his work shift that afternoon he'd noticed that a flyer for a weekend concert by Peter Pines, a former rock performer now famous for his children's CDs, had been replaced by an announcement for a lesbian dance. Alongside the usual advertisements for music lessons, and children's party performers, and pilates classes for expectant mothers, there were new notices about meetings to protest the big construction projects threatening to change the nature of the neighborhood — or so their authors felt. Since Paul's plans didn't include living in the area permanently, the meetings didn't interest him. As he stepped toward the narrow staircase that would take him to the co-op office to sign in, the entry door opened and a tall, unsmiling man in his mid-forties stepped in. Not bad-looking, broad-chested but slender otherwise, and obviously fit. Moving quickly toward the bulletin board, the man swung his backpack to the floor and withdrew a handful of flyers and a card of thumbtacks.

Paul didn't know why, but he stayed on, watching. Or, rather, he did understand what kept him, but was too embarrassed to admit the source of his continued interest, even to himself. Stoutly apolitical, he nonetheless couldn't shake a sense of loyalty to the notice for the lesbian dance, and found himself looking on with rising tension to see if the stranger meant to shift it to a less visible position in order to make room for his own announcement.

"Do you know if there's anywhere I can leave extra copies?"

"Oh, uh — no, I don't think there is," said Paul, startled by the unexpected appeal. He thought of directing the man to the office, but changed his mind. He hadn't been a food co-op member all that long. It might be better to find out what the policy was, regarding the placement of flyers, before giving out advice.

"Here, why don't you take one," the man said glumly, passing a

at home anywhere

copy to Paul before tossing the rest into the backpack. "Maybe you know someone who can help me out." Paul stared at the sheet and read:

"HANDY"MAN
"Clean" "Honest" "Hardworking" "Fully" Employed
Seeks Immediate Share or Apartment in Park Slope.
Must Allow Pets!

The customary fringe of detachable telephone numbers completed the page.

"I don't know of anyplace offhand," Paul murmured, wondering at the text's curious punctuation. Didn't the man know that by placing quotes around the words "hardworking" and "honest," he created the impression that there was something dubious about his claims? For that matter, why did he feel the need to advertise such characteristics in the first place, except from uncertainty?

"Well, I hope you'll keep me in mind," the man said. "The name's Tyler. Tyler Landry." Then he paused, as though expecting Paul to say something appreciative. But Paul only replied: "Sure thing," and was relieved when the stranger finally turned to go.

He must be desperate, Paul thought, pocketing the flyer and recalling his own frantic search for an affordable room. Climbing the stairs to the office to get his work assignment, he remembered days when he'd honestly thought he might end up like the men at SHARE — Self-Help-And-REspect — the local soup kitchen where he volunteered four times a week serving meals to the homeless, among whom there was no dearth of honest, hard-working, uncared-for men.

Once his shift started, Paul thought no more about the handyman. He bagged raisins for an hour and then he was assigned to stocking shelves with seltzer. When his shift ended he did his own shopping, purchasing aduki beans, organic spinach, honey, rice milk, brown rice, and a block of Parmesan cheese.

He walked home along Sixth Avenue rather than Seventh in order to quiet his mind. He had visited the commercial strip the day before. Sonia had called to ask him to stop at the copy shop to pick up the postcards advertising her latest book, which had just been published by the ashram she belonged to. It was called: *Free/FeMale/Me: A Journey of Hope and Healing*. Paul performed such duties, along with dog care, light housekeeping, and payment of a modest rent, in exchange for a large basement room in Sonia's house.

"We're in luck," Sonia said as she re-entered the house from the garden. "He's free this evening. I thought that would be the best way for us to get to know him better and see if we're compatible."

"Great," Paul replied, finding comfort in her use of the plurals *us* and *we*. "I'll cook. I got some really nice spinach at the co-op. I was going to make an aduki bean casserole and a spinach salad."

"That sounds wonderful."

"What time did you ask him for?"

"Eight o'clock."

"Well, if you're going to be in until then, I can get the aduki beans started, and finish everything when I come back from Mass."

"That's fine. I'll keep an eye on them. I'm not going out again."

He stood up. Sonia aimed the remote at the television and the set came on, signaling that he was dismissed.

Paul had just placed a bowl of tahini dip in the center of the coffee table when the doorbell rang. Sonia went to answer it. Through the gate, the visitor said, "I brought my dog, Teddy. I hope you don't mind. If they don't get along, there's no point in our talking." The voice, rich and deep, sounded even more melancholy than Paul remembered.

A rust-colored dog trotted into the room. Sonia followed, and then Tyler, towering over her. "That's Teddy," Tyler said.

"You know Paul," Sonia said, smiling. Tyler extended his hand. "Sure," he replied, sounding only a little puzzled at the warmth of her introduction; "Paul."

"Please sit down," said Sonia. Tyler complied, settling uneasily into a chair.

"If you'll excuse me, I'm wanted in the kitchen," Paul quipped. "Can I get you anything to drink?"

"I'll have some wine," Sonia replied. "Tyler, would you like something?"

"Uh, no thanks," said Tyler, sitting forward, stiffly, "Well, maybe just some water."

at home anywhere

Returning with the water and Sonia's wine a few minutes later, Paul heard Tyler explain Teddy's pedigree. He was a mix of Chow and Springer Spaniel, younger than the other dogs and understandably more playful. Finn and Mischa soon abandoned the newcomer for their usual places, Mischa under the piano and Finn near the wall. But Luke and Teddy continued to romp. As Paul entered the living room to announce the start of dinner, both dogs crashed into the coffee table and he suggested Luke spend some time downstairs.

"I'm sorry," Tyler apologized, defeatedly, seeming convinced that he would soon be asked to leave. "I'll take Teddy home."

"It's all right, my room is down there," Paul quickly replied. "Luke won't mind if it's just for an hour." Instantly, he regretted his effort to reassure their guest. It suddenly seemed unwise to keep Sonia in the dark about how little he knew Tyler Landry. It wasn't too late to confess. She might be angry or "disappointed," as she would put it, that he hadn't been entirely honest about their acquaintance, but that wouldn't last very long. Certainly not as long as the fallout from inviting Tyler Landry into their home if he turned out to be a jerk, or even dangerous, wanted in six states for doing some kind of violence to people he'd just met.

Tyler called Teddy to his side. The dog obeyed, and Paul led a whimpering Luke out of the room.

When he returned, Sonia and Tyler had moved from the living room at the front of the house, to the dining room at the rear. They were already seated at the table, an antique oak with flowers carved into the sides, illuminated by a stained glass lamp. "This is nice," Tyler said, taking in the glass wall at the rear of the house. At that hour, Sonia's garden was only a dark promise, breathing beyond their bright reflections in the windows. He had brought wine, which Paul opened and poured.

"You're a waiter, aren't you?" Tyler asked.

"Yes," said Paul.

"I was a waiter myself in Dallas. I recognize the moves."

"Is that where you are from?" Sonia asked.

"That's right," he replied, and that was the beginning of the real work of the evening, which was to find out who Tyler Landry was.

His place of origin was the only fact Tyler volunteered. Not that he seemed evasive. He willingly answered their questions, with a modest,

62

Felix and adauctus

self-effacing manner. He had learned carpentry after he quit serving. Joined the union in Dallas. Decided he really wanted to see New York, so when a carpenter acquaintance announced he was going north, Tyler joined him.

"The wages are better here, I guess," said Sonia, and Tyler fell right into the trap.

"You bet! I can make double here what I can in Texas."

And why was he looking for a place to live now?

Too late, he realized where she was leading him. A union carpenter in the city that was "constantly rebuilding itself," to borrow a phrase from a television commercial; how had he come to be begging for a share to live in at this point in his life?

"I've been living with my girlfriend for the past two years," he replied, with obvious reluctance. "She has a daughter. She just never liked me. The daughter, I mean. Which I understand. I mean, kids don't want to share their mother with a stranger. Let's face it."

"Is that who made your sign?" Sonia gently inquired.

"What? Oh, the flyer. That's right. She has a computer at work," Tyler explained, adding: "I haven't had time to learn about computers. I'm too busy earning a living." Paul remembered the quotation marks around certain words on the flyer, and wondered if they might be the maker's attempt at a warning.

"So, she's trying to help you," Sonia said, sympathetically.

"Well, yeah," said Tyler, frowning, as though surprised to find his girlfriend still the topic of conversation when the meeting was supposed to be about him.

Paul cleared the table, declining Tyler's offer of assistance, and served dessert: bread pudding made with rice milk. Sonia began to clarify the terms of tenancy.

Tyler had to understand that he couldn't bring any furniture with him. The room, which she would show him when they finished this excellent bread pudding (nod and smile towards Paul), was already furnished. Sonia had removed her daughter's personal belongings, but the furniture would stay. "That's fine," said Tyler, the desperate look returning to his features. Paul thought he must have realized that his cause had apparently advanced, and that any mistake would be more costly now than at the start of the evening. Sonia went on: as he could imagine a house of this

at home anywhere

age and size needed a certain amount of upkeep; she was often out of town and had unfortunately neglected it for quite some time.

Paul was surprised at how quickly Tyler's attention flagged past this point. He was still very agreeable, nodding at appropriate intervals. But his gaze wandered, first to the antique frames hung on the exposed-brick wall behind his head: photos of Sonia's daughters in school and on family vacations to the Galapagos and Costa Rica. Then to the plants along the ledge between the dining room and patio, the track lighting around the perimeter of the room, the custom-built island separating the kitchen from the dining room, the terra-cotta tiled floor. Perhaps Sonia thought Tyler's interest was professional, that he was carrying on his own appraisal as they spoke. Paul wondered if he could be casing the joint, but then realized that anyone with larceny in mind would try to conceal his roving focus. For his part he hoped Tyler had already decided that he didn't want to move in, and therefore didn't care what Sonia thought of his manners. But when Sonia suggested they view the room, Tyler jumped eagerly to his feet. "Let's do it," he said.

Paul considered following them upstairs when they left to examine the available bedroom. And more importantly, the bathroom they all shared, lined with hand-made Italian tile that had to be wiped down and dried after every shower to prevent the build-up of ruinous scum. Sonia was very particular about that tile.

He would leave it in God's hands, he thought, finally, reversing direction at the foot of the stairs to return to the kitchen and wash up, whether or not Tyler Landry returned.

"What do you think?" Sonia inquired, when Tyler and Teddy were gone.

"He seems fine," said Paul. "The dog is well-trained."

"Yes, that's important. I'm actually impressed that he thought of bringing Teddy. He's right, when you think of it. Even if we had all decided we were compatible, we couldn't consider having him here if the dogs weren't."

"So you are going to offer him the room?" Paul asked, keeping his voice carefully neutral while his thoughts flew. Should he confess that he had met Tyler for the first time only that afternoon? Or make the case that he should have been considered first for the upstairs room, and new-

Felix and adauctus

comer Tyler offered the one in the basement? The issue was complicated. Sonia would not appreciate being put into the position of having to notify Tyler of the change. Tyler could reasonably protest that he'd been tricked, and Paul had to agree that on the surface it looked like a classic bait and switch operation: show the prospective tenant a light-filled room initially, then call back with the word that it wasn't available after all, but another, less attractive one was. Sonia might also resent the unspoken reproach Paul's request contained: what did it say about her sensitivity, a big part of her professional identity, that she hadn't thought to offer him Emma's room first? It might be best to yield to the newcomer. In fact, it was the perfect penance for passing Tyler off as a food co-op regular.

"Well, I'm going to call his references. He gave me the number at his union. I feel a little uncomfortable about calling his girlfriend, but he gave me her number too."

"It sounds like they're still friendly."

"Yes, it does. Anyway, as soon as I've talked to them, I'll let him know when he can move in."

Sonia seemed very pleased to report, the next afternoon, that Tyler Landry's references checked out. He was indeed a union member. His girlfriend seemed resigned to the breakup, not cheerful of course, but not hostile: "She said they just don't make each other happy anymore."

That night Sonia was called out of town to replace a speaker at a personal empowerment seminar in Vermont, which meant that she wouldn't be present when Tyler moved in. Paul assured her that he would make himself available to Tyler while he got settled. She left a list of the repairs she wanted undertaken, explaining that she had already discussed them with Tyler in general terms and would have liked to walk him through them herself, but there wasn't time, so the list would have to do. Paul promised to pass it on.

She was gone for over an hour when Paul realized that he didn't know precisely when Tyler was supposed to arrive. He thought of calling, but Sonia hadn't left a number where she could be reached. She hadn't left the flyer with Tyler's number on it, either. So he spent a day and a half in a curious state of suspense. He had just recovered fully from the stress of his own move, and now things were changing again. A

65

at home anywhere

stranger in the house, more frequently at home than Sonia was. He wished it was all over with, Tyler installed upstairs, everything about what that would mean already known, good and bad. He completed all his chores: vacuumed the first floor and the stairs, walked and fed the dogs, copied the messages on the answering machine into the book Sonia kept for that purpose. But he was preoccupied, and the dogs noticed. Luke, especially, seemed agitated, and had to be taken out alone. That made him late for his Thursday shift at SHARE. Finally, early Friday morning, Tyler called to ask when it would be convenient to come. He sounded even more dispirited than he had the first time they'd met. "Anytime," Paul said, glad the uncertainty was nearly at an end. "I go to Mass at four o'clock, and then I go to work. Anytime before that is fine."

Paul was watering the plants at the front of the living room when Tyler Landry drove up in a station wagon crammed with his belongings. Parting the lace curtains for a better look, he wondered how accountable Sonia would hold *him* for Tyler's apparent disregard of the first condition of his tenancy: that he come without furniture?

On the way to the door Paul scolded himself. Maybe Tyler was just stopping to leave his clothing off before carting his furniture on to one of those self-storage places. But when Paul reached the street he saw that Tyler had already unloaded an eight foot bookcase from the roof of the car and was in the process of untying another. It was a warm day and Tyler wore no jacket. His shirt rose above his slender hips as he reached his arms around the bookcase. Tossing the ropes into the back of the car, he slid the bookcase onto his back and started towards the house, not speaking until he had set it down alongside the stairs.

"She here?" Tyler asked, grimly, resting his hands on his hips. His fingers were long and shapely, the nails straight and clean.

"Sonia? No."

"Good. Think you can give me a hand getting my stuff inside?"

That would have been the moment to inquire if Tyler had forgotten Sonia's directive. Or to ask Tyler to wait a few minutes while he tried to figure out a way to warn her about his noncompliance. But there had settled around him a sensation of sudden intimacy, as though the scene underway had been performed before. Paul recalled childhood episodes of déjà vu, when he and his brothers enacted some eerily

Felix and adauctus

familiar vignette. The incidents pleased him, seeming to suggest an other-worldly bond: they must have been together in a different time and place. The sensation had grown increasingly rare as he got older, and he found himself unwilling to do anything to discourage it today.

"Which end do you want to take?" Tyler inquired.

"The back, I think," Paul replied. Tyler motioned him forward. Upon switching places, their hands brushed and Paul's ears burned. As Tyler backed into the house, Paul recalled the time some members of the high school football team beat up his lover so badly that the boy lost his sight in one eye. Their violence was necessary, they later explained: the boy was a fucking queer, a faggot, a frequent flyer on the Hershey Highway. The same mix of fear and desire those boys had aroused in Paul flooded him now. He had sometimes thought that if the only way they would touch him was to hurt him then he almost wished they would.

The first bookcase fit between the windows in Tyler's bedroom, and Paul thought that if that had been the only piece he came with, Sonia probably wouldn't have minded. But in addition to the second bookcase there were half a dozen milk crates; a rolling clothes rack and a very large, very dirty yellow armchair. Tyler handled those, leaving Paul to scurry up and down the stairs with lamps and boxes of records and tapes and stereo components.

The chair was the last thing Tyler carried in, and Paul found him sitting in it when he returned with the final carton. "This is it," he said, looking around for a place to put the box. Whatever grace the room had before was gone.

"You lock the car?" asked Tyler.

Paul nodded.

"Thanks for the help."

"No problem. Where's Teddy?"

"I'm going to get him right now," said Tyler, heaving himself out of the chair.

Paul followed him downstairs, passing on to the kitchen while Tyler went outside. Then he remembered that he was supposed to give Tyler the house keys, which Sonia had left with the repair list in a small hand-thrown bowl that she'd moved to the center of the counter. Snatching up the keys, he ran after Tyler, reaching the doorway just as a woman

at home anywhere

approached from Seventh Avenue, with Teddy alongside. The woman had dark hair and a long nose. She held out her hand. Tyler surrendered a set of keys; the woman handed over Teddy. And Tyler was theirs.

Paul heard Tyler call something after the woman as she walked away, but didn't wait to see if she turned around. Hurrying back to the kitchen, he replaced the keys inside the bowl, and descended to his room. He thought Tyler might want some privacy at a time like this. Half an hour later, when he left for Mass, he heard Teddy pawing at the inside of Tyler's door. He considered knocking to see if Tyler was home, but reasoned that might upset the dog even more. So he left, as quietly as possible.

If he had spoken to Tyler before leaving, Paul would have mentioned that Teddy didn't need to be confined to his room. Later, he realized that Tyler must have drawn that conclusion on his own, because while there was no sign of Tyler on the first floor when he got home, Teddy came forward with the other dogs at the sound of his key in the lock.

After greeting the dogs he went into the kitchen. Evidently Tyler had found the keys, because the only thing left in the bowl was the repair list. The shower was running upstairs. He usually took the dogs out for a short walk before going to bed, and wondered if Teddy needed walking, too.

He climbed the stairs and knocked at the door to the bathroom. "Tyler?"

No answer.

"Tyler, it's me, Paul. Can you hear me?"

"Wait! Hold on!" Tyler shouted. A moment later the door opened, and Paul watched a pink and lathered Tyler jump back into the shower and slide the door closed.

Paul stared at the floor as he spoke, acutely conscious of the rosy form moving behind the frosted glass. "I just wanted to know, does Teddy need a walk? I was about to go out."

"I walked all of them half an hour ago!"

"Mischa too?"

"Yeah! He only made it once around the block, though!"

"Great. Thanks."

"No problem!" The door slid open. Tyler stuck out his head. "Maybe we can work something out," he said. "Take turns." All traces of his earlier melancholy were gone.

"Sure," he said. "Goodnight. Thanks again." Just before leaving

Felix and adauctus

the room he weakened, glancing back to catch another glimpse of Tyler under glass.

Even though he slept alone, Paul readied himself for bed in the dark, as he had when he'd shared a room with three brothers. At home the darkened room created a protective privacy, a rare thing in a large family of small means. At the same time, the dark brought him closer to his brothers, asleep under the same pilled blankets, breathing the same cold air. In daylight his difference made closeness impossible, though nothing was ever said, and they never teased him. Two of his brothers were goths in high school, and one was a sci-fi freak, so they were all the targets of jock disdain.

As he lay back against the pillow, he considered Tyler's resemblance to the wealthy boys back home. Since coming to the city he'd learned to distinguish many more grades of affluence than he'd known about before. In retrospect he realized the town boys were probably only middle class, but from where his family sat, they'd seemed rich. He recalled the unspoken ideal: narrow hips, legs of every type outlined by their pressed, plumb-straight leg jeans or chinos. The best feet were narrow, with a high arch. Some of the boys wore moccasin-type loafers, without socks in summertime, so you could see that even their feet were tanned. Unlike his own broad bloodless feet, that were so hard to fit for shoes. As though the others were meant to skim through life and his kind to plod.

So the question was: how did someone made like a skimmer come to be plodding alongside him in Sonia Fisher's house?

Monday was Paul's night off from the restaurant. Before leaving for Mass, he told Tyler that he had cooked, and to please help himself to lentil soup if he felt hungry. But when he returned two hours later, Tyler was clearing away the remains of a take-out meal. Paul recognized the red plastic bag one of the local restaurants used. "I see you went to Zen," he said. "What did you think of the food?"

"It's good. But they're expensive. I found the menu right here on the refrigerator so I thought you must order from them a lot. How come they're so expensive?" Tyler asked.

Pleased by the appeal for information, Paul began to frame an answer. "I guess it's because..." He was going to say that high quality ingredients cost more, but Tyler interrupted:

"How come you go to Mass so much?"

Paul started to reply: "I go to Mass because I think I want to..." Enter a religious order at some point, he was about to go on, but Tyler was off again:

"When she's here, does she expect you to cook for her?"

"By 'she' I assume you mean Sonia," Paul said, coolly, unwilling to continue to address Tyler's questions when he showed so little interest in the answers.

"Well yeah! Who do you think I mean, one of the dogs?" Tyler exclaimed, widening his eyes in a manner Paul thought likely was meant to be comical. So he smiled.

"No. But I always ask her to join me when I cook. Sometimes she does."

"How often? Half the time? Three quarters of the time?"

"About half the time. Actually, since I moved in..." he began, intending to explain that Sonia hadn't been around all that much, but Tyler had already moved on to another topic:

"Speaking of the dogs, how long have you had Luke?"

Had they been speaking of the dogs? Paul wondered, but as Tyler would be walking Luke from time to time, it seemed a good idea to take the opportunity to discuss him. "I've had him almost a year. I got him from an animal shelter. He'd been abused."

"Oh, that explains a lot. Earlier I just tied him and Teddy up so I could go into the liquor store..."

"And he started howling?"

"Yeah! I've never heard anything like it. I had to leave the store!"

"At the shelter they said he was tied up outside constantly. In all weather, without food for long periods."

"He is awful skinny."

"Oh, he's gained weight since I got him. The people at the shelter said they rescued him just in time; he would have starved to death within days."

He recognized the sin of vanity that made him anticipate Tyler's praise, which usually ran along the lines of *lucky for him you showed up*, or *you must really love dogs*, and prepared himself not to enjoy it. But he was disappointed: Tyler made no reference to Paul's role in Luke's rescue.

Felix and adauctus

"Well," Tyler said, contentedly, placing his glass in the sink, "I guess I'll go upstairs and take my shower."

"Oh! I almost forgot," Paul exclaimed, suddenly remembering the terms of Tyler's habitation. "Before you go — in that bowl there, the blue one? Sonia left a list of the projects she'd like you to work on. She said you already discussed them before she left."

"Thanks," said Tyler, glancing at the bowl. "I'll uh, I'll come down and take a look at it later."

Paul opened the refrigerator and stared in, shifting dishes for effect as Tyler moved away, turning in time to see him swallowed up by the shadow on the stairs: first his head and shoulders, then hips and legs, finally the feet, noting that his toes turned in slightly. Facing the sink, he scrubbed the potatoes he had retrieved from the crisper with unusual vigor. What made it so exciting to catch someone in a lie? he wondered. His heart beat as though he'd witnessed a burglary, and all because he realized that Tyler had absolutely no intention of coming down later to look at the list.

Two days later, the list remained where Sonia had placed it. Tyler came in at noon. He seemed angry, complaining, as he withdrew a bottle of wine from the refrigerator, "They only send out the guys with connections. You've got to have a godfather to work in New York. Do they think I don't notice?"

Paul allowed a minute to pass before speaking. "I'm going — out," he said, carefully avoiding the word 'work'. "Have you had a chance to look at the list Sonia left?"

Tyler frowned.

"She called today and asked how the repairs were going."

Tyler's frown deepened, but he reached into the bowl and withdrew the list, printed in clear block letters on a sheet torn from a lined yellow pad. After a quick glance he grunted, then dropped the sheet back into the bowl.

"Are you going to leave it there?" Paul asked.

"Why not?"

"I just thought you might need it to — well, to order materials."

"Oh, I probably have everything I'll need," Tyler replied, moving towards the refrigerator to replace the bottle of wine. "So, when will you

71

be back?" he asked.

"Around midnight. I'm going to the restaurant after SHARE," Paul replied.

"Don't worry about the dogs. I'll walk 'em," Tyler said.

Paul thought, *I should protest*. He didn't want to be in Tyler's debt, but couldn't see how to avoid being cooperative, at least where the dogs were concerned. His unease would be too obvious if he asked Tyler to leave the other dogs home when he took out Teddy. So he settled for making plain his intention to keep up his end: "I'll take them out when I get back."

"No problem."

"Great. Thanks," Paul said. And left, glad to be on his way to work, where he'd be too busy to think about any of this for hours.

Paul liked to get off the train a stop early and walk uptown along Madison Avenue the rest of the way to Les Trois Oiseaux. Popular with local people as well as visitors, the restaurant was a series of beautifully furnished small rooms, each one decorated with antiques from a different period, just visible to the diners in the other rooms through a clever arrangement of internal windows, floral arrangements, mirrors and screens.

He didn't think it was only because he'd come to know some of the regulars among the clientele that Madison Avenue seemed so familiar, more like the main drag in an affluent town than the city's other big streets. Or maybe more accurately like what someone from a small town would imagine a big street in New York to be like. What he had expected the entire city to be like, in fact, despite all the television shows about hardened cops and lawyers. It felt safe, in a way that Broadway and Fifth Avenue didn't always, and that was why he felt so at home when he came up the street from the subway.

Two blocks from the restaurant, Paul paused in front of a shoe store. He had been walking on the opposite side of the street for the last two weeks to avoid the store. Not that he could afford the shoes displayed in the windows of Egoiste. Just seeing them was so pleasurable, however, that he felt even visual abstinence offered the opportunity for spiritual enrichment. Tyler's presence in his life had weakened his resolve: Tyler's narrow feet at the bottom of his stovepipe jeans, like the rich boys back

Felix and adauctus

home. Had their feet been so important because that was where Paul instinctively cast his gaze when they were near? Hoping to escape their attention, which, once aroused, was never friendly. He hadn't known how much he loved shoes until he came to New York. Until he saw this small shop, in fact. No need for shouting advertisements, or "sale" signs. Pulling in passers-by simply wasn't necessary. A wooden foot, amputated at the ankle, sat inside each pair. Fashioned of burnished leather, the shoes featured elegantly sculpted heels; tassels hung off some of the styles like ripe fruit. There'd be no question of your taste or your station in life in a pair of shoes from Egoiste. And Paul felt as though the little card tucked into one corner of the window spoke directly to him: *We Fit the Hard to Fit*. Well, today he would indulge himself, and spend a few moments looking in. Tomorrow and for the remainder of the week he could leave home a little later and take the subway all the way to work, forgoing the pleasure of window-shopping altogether to make up for his fall today.

Paul dated his vocation from the time in high school when a visiting priest befriended his family. His brothers had already stopped attending Mass by the time Father Ernie was posted to their parish. Paul's mother still tried to make it to the one o'clock Mass at St. Peter's before the offertory on Sunday — the last service that could be counted towards her weekly obligation — and Paul made it seem as though he only continued the practice for her sake. She didn't like entering the church alone, and he told his brothers that he didn't have the heart to refuse her. In fact he still felt the same compulsion to go as he had when he was younger, and thought it would hurt God's feelings if he stayed away. And God — who *was* the bloodied Jesus on the cross at the front of the church — had suffered enough.

Unlike the regular priests of the parish, who never came off the altar once they told the assembly to "Go in peace," Father Ernie waited outside after Mass to talk to people. For the first few weeks the parishioners evaded him. Paul overheard one woman say, "What does he think, we're Protestants?" But little by little they warmed to the new

at home anywhere

custom. It was pleasant to greet Father Ernie, who clasped their hands between his big paws while he smiled into their faces and made small talk. Paul's mother persisted in avoiding the priest longer than most others, but eventually Father Ernie captured her as well. "Mrs. Kosciak, isn't it?" he said one morning at the start of Lent, leaning into the stream of people exiting the church to single her out. "Can I ask you a favor?"

A little knot of people were waiting on the priest's notice, and some didn't disguise their annoyance when Father Ernie bypassed them to draw his mother into his orbit.

"I've been asking the other priests if they knew a family that could help me with one of my projects, and your name came up. Is this your son?"

Nervously, Paul's mother filled in the family tree: "I got a husband and three other sons at home, but this is the only one I could get to come with me; the rest of 'em are too lazy!" She often joked when she was anxious or embarrassed, and the novelty of the priest's attention had made her both. She tossed her head in Paul's direction and Father Ernie followed her gaze. The lore that accompanied his arrival in the parish included that he had been a marine, and after that a missionary, and those experiences were offered as the explanation for his military haircut, his straightforward preaching style, and these meetings on the church steps after Mass. He began to describe his project: he had donations of clothing that needed to be boxed up to send to missions overseas; was Paul interested? He couldn't pay much, but there would be some compensation. His mother demurred; of course Father shouldn't think of paying Paul, who would be happy to help out. Paul stood looking on, smiling, knowing it would break his mother's heart if he refused, but hopeful the priest would insist on paying him for the work. It was arranged that Paul would stop by the rectory the next afternoon at four.

When Paul arrived the following day Father Ernie was polite but distant, almost as though he had forgotten about the invitation, or that something more important had come up in the meantime. After Paul reminded him of their meeting outside the church, the priest showed him to the basement, where piles of clothes were stacked in every corner; more clean, wrinkled clothes than Paul had ever seen. Most had never been worn, and store labels hung from the sleeves or necklines. Father Ernie said that Paul should sort the clothes into four piles: for girl and boy

Felix and adauctus

children, and male and female adults. Then he was to box them, again keeping the categories separate. The priest showed Paul the flattened boxes and how they should be taped, and what had to be written on the front, and then he went back upstairs. The furnace was blasting away on one side of the basement and the small windows at the front of the space wouldn't open, so after a while Paul removed his shirt. He had filled a dozen boxes when Father Ernie returned with a Coke and a hot dog. Boiled, in a cold bun, with cold mustard on top, the same way his mother served them.

While Paul sat and ate, Father Ernie crossed his hands against a beam overhead. Then, resting his forehead on his hands, he started asking questions: where did Paul go to school, and what did he want to do after he graduated — that kind of thing. At the time Paul thought he would like to be an architect; he'd gotten an A in the mechanical drawing class at school. The priest was easy to talk to and Paul told him things he hadn't told anyone else: about how he hadn't mentioned becoming an architect to either of his parents yet because his mother had enough to worry about with a husband who drank all the time and couldn't keep a job. And how the teachers at school would probably be surprised to hear that he wanted to be an architect because they formed their opinions about people based on the family they came from. After hearing Paul's reply Father Ernie asked what he thought the teachers expected him to become?

"Best case? Military. More likely a custodian at the nursing home." That had been his father's latest job. Of course he didn't tell the priest that he was gay.

When Paul finished the hot dog he got up and grabbed another box, but the priest told him it was time to "call it a day." Paul put his shirt back on and followed Father Ernie upstairs, trying not to let his anxiety about the money show in his face. At the door the priest turned around and pulled out his wallet. He gave Paul ten dollars. All the while he was working in the hot basement Paul had been trying to decide what amount he should be offered. At times his estimation went as high as twenty-five dollars, but he was relieved when Father Ernie pressed the more modest amount into his hand. Now he could take or leave the job; he didn't feel beholden.

at home anywhere

    A few nights later Father Ernie called the house to ask if Paul thought he could come to work for him again. His mother took the call. Once again she volunteered Paul's time without asking him first. He decided that he didn't mind — he'd enjoyed his conversation with the priest. After that he went to the rectory a few more times once school ended for the day, until the basement was full. Then Father Ernie started to bring clothes and flattened boxes over to Paul's house on Saturday mornings. He'd stay on in the kitchen talking to Paul's mother after dropping everything off. One time she admired a blouse that dropped to the floor as the priest carried in a pile of clothing, and when she picked it up he told her to keep it. It took a lot to convince her to accept the blouse; she said she felt guilty taking clothing from people in one of those countries you saw on TV where they really had nothing. But Father Ernie said there was no shortage of the clothes. He got them from a former candidate for the priesthood who had decided the religious life wasn't for him and now worked for one of the big discount department stores down in New York City; he sent everything left unsold at the end of the season to Father Ernie to ship overseas.

    From that point on Paul's mother got first pick of all the women's things, and with the priest's encouragement began taking some garments for the rest of the family as well. But it was obvious they were coming to the end of their work. It now rarely took more than half an hour to fill the boxes Father Ernie brought to the house. Sometimes the priest was still sitting in the kitchen when Paul finished. Then Father Ernie carried the boxes out to his car and drove away. Paul never asked him whether he had mailed any of the clothes, or where the boxes were stored until they were sent overseas.

    After that Father Ernie started dropping by once or twice a week, later in the afternoon, even when he didn't bring any clothing to sort and box. Sometimes he was already there when Paul and his brothers came home from school. During the first visit, when Paul's mother rose to go to work, the priest rose with her. She motioned him back into his seat. "Don't run out just because I have to go. Finish your coffee." His brothers never stuck around, but Paul usually stayed on in the kitchen after his mother left. Father Ernie had been in Korea and Japan and a couple of other places, and he told some pretty interesting stories about the people

Felix and adauctus

he'd met. He'd been stopping in for a couple of months when school closed for the Easter break, and he invited Paul on a camping trip. He told Paul's mother the weekend was partly a reward for all Paul's hard work getting the clothes ready to ship for the missions. He was taking another kid from the parish, too, a twelve-year-old whose father had recently died; somebody Paul didn't know. Father Ernie thought being with someone a little older like Paul might cheer the other boy up.

Paul's mother gave her permission and right after Easter Father Ernie drove the boys to a cabin on a lake about two hours away. He said the cabin belonged to an old friend of his. Paul thought Michael, the other boy, was all right, though it was hard to tell much about him because he was so quiet. When they arrived they spent an hour cleaning up the mouse droppings that were everywhere in the kitchen. Then they made bologna sandwiches, and after that they took a hike to a small waterfall. Back at the cabin they ate again, sloppy joes, and then they played Gin Rummy until Michael asked if he could go to bed.

The cabin was big enough for each to have his own room, and after everyone had been in bed about an hour the priest came into Paul's room. "Are you awake?" he said, and switched on the light. Paul turned over to face the door and saw that Father Ernie was holding out one of those life-sized inflatable dolls.

"Hey, look who just showed up!" he went on, pretending the doll was dancing toward Paul's bed. "What do you think? Do you like her?"

Paul's first instinct was to kick the doll away and shout *what kind of weirdo are you?* Did Father Ernie intend the doll to loosen him up, get him talking about the things he did with girls? Or was it meant to make him reveal an interest in boys that the priest already suspected? The same way the jocks at school pushed pages torn from pornographic magazines into his face when he walked through the locker room after gym? He felt betrayed, as though all their conversations were only a ploy to get him to confess to something. But he put on the placid expression he used to deflect attention at school. "Where'd that come from?" he said, mildly, shifting his weight when Father Ernie placed the doll alongside him on the bed. She was pale pink under her baby-blue bathing suit, with a cartoon face; not very life-like.

"I saw her in that last gas station we stopped at," the priest replied,

at home anywhere

and Paul heard the panic running under his voice, and that made him think that Father Ernie might not know exactly what he intended the doll to do. He recalled the way the priest had sounded at the Stations of the Cross service a few days earlier, describing Christ's wounds — almost moved to tears. And then at the Easter service Paul attended with his mother, when Father Ernie reminded the congregation that Jesus had saved his most important message for last: Forgive.

"Maybe tomorrow we can see if she floats," Paul said, with a little laugh, tossing the doll to the bottom of the bed; not angrily, not fearfully; but just as he would have tossed aside an inoffensive swimming ring.

Relief flooded the priest's expression. "That's what I was thinking," he said.

When Paul woke up the next morning the doll had been removed, and no one mentioned it again. The rest of the trip passed uneventfully. Father Ernie was a little subdued. But Michael started to relax; he talked more and more as the priest talked less. When it was time to drive back, Paul realized that the trip had fulfilled the goal Father Ernie had described to his mother. He was able to report to Mrs. Kosciak, truthfully, that Paul had been very helpful: Michael was considerably more cheerful returning than he had been going out.

Not long after that Father Ernie announced from the pulpit that he had been called to help in another parish. Outside after Mass he told Paul's mother that he wouldn't be shipping any more clothes overseas for the foreseeable future. He clasped her hands in his and thanked her for her hospitality, and then he turned to Paul and made the sign of the cross on his forehead and blessed him. Paul liked to think the priest moved on so as not to fall into an occasion of sin. And not because he was afraid that Paul might tell his mother, or some other adult, about the doll on the camping trip. Paul never had told her, or anyone else, and in fact he was grateful to Father Ernie, because he marked that night in the cabin as the inspiration for his calling to the religious life. He'd seen the priest's weakness and desire, but he hadn't let that frighten him. He'd waited, and that gave Father Ernie the chance to catch himself in time. Wasn't everyone a mix of good and bad impulses? Through a small act of mercy he'd been able to help a good man. He wanted to spend his life that way.

Felix and Adauctus

Filled with inspired repentance from his stop at the Egoiste shoe store, Paul was exceptionally quick serving his section that night. And remarkably patient, even with the elderly woman whose son dropped her off each evening while he went to dine elsewhere, and who always wanted something not on the menu, and then wondered aloud, frequently and querulously while waiting for it to be prepared, why others who had arrived later were being served sooner. Even with the well-known models and their handlers, who claimed that the temperature in the first two rooms they occupied was uneven, with the people on one side of the table complaining of cold and those on the other of uncomfortable warmth. "You're a saint," the maître 'd said, after Paul had moved the group for the second time, willingly fitting them out with new place settings since they couldn't be expected to carry their own cutlery and table linen from one room to the other, and bringing fresh appetizers, though they'd already encroached upon the ones at the other tables. Paul smiled. "Hardly," he said.

But his colleague's comment reminded him of the *Penguin Dictionary of Saints* that lay at the bottom of his backpack. He hadn't opened it in some time. On the subway ride home he read the short history of Felix and Adauctus. Eternally linked in martyrdom, the two met only as Felix was being led to his execution through the streets of Rome. An onlooker was so moved by the scene that he cried out: "I am also a Christian, and I too would die for Christ." At which point he was promptly seized and led away to join Felix in death. There wasn't time to discover his real name, so his biographers called him Adauctus— "The Additional One."

Closing the book Paul considered what meaning Adauctus' sacrifice might have for him. He decided that the martyr was an example of the potential spiritual power of even brief associations. His sainthood showed that acts of impulse could move the individual towards grace as surely as an entire life of sacrifice, provided the stakes were sufficiently grave.

At home only Teddy and Luke came forward to greet him. Mischa and Finn looked up, but didn't stir.

at home anywhere

Just one of the track lights was on in the kitchen, aimed, coincidentally, at the little blue bowl with Sonia's list of chores for Tyler inside. Paul touched a finger to the paper, worrying again about what Sonia would expect his role to be should Tyler continue to ignore his duties. Naturally they had not discussed the possibility. At his interview Tyler had seemed so earnest, so willing. As long as Tyler fulfilled his early promise, his own part in bringing the newcomer into their midst would go unremarked. But if something went wrong, Sonia would surely be reminded: Paul had brought Tyler's flyer home.

It was too late to do anything about it now, he thought, withdrawing his hand. He would take a shower and think about Tyler in the morning.

Ten minutes later, someone knocked at the bathroom door. Paul stopped the water. "Yes? What is it?"

"Hey, Paul, if you have a minute, come into my room when you're finished, will ya?"

He wondered if something was wrong. Or perhaps Tyler was ready to discuss the list.

"Sure," he said, turning the water back on, relieved.

Still, he was wary, knocking at the door to Tyler's room with some misgiving. The restaurant had been very busy that night. He hoped whatever Tyler had to say about the list would be brief.

The door swung open. Behind it stood Tyler, looking tousled and sleepy, holding a glass of wine. On the periphery of his vision, Paul noticed that his narrow feet were bare.

"C'mon in," Tyler said, standing aside. "Can I get you some wine?"

"No thanks. It'll keep me awake and I'm really tired."

"Have a seat," Tyler said, pointing to the dirty armchair. "There, you can have that chair right there."

"This is fine," Paul declined, sitting on a folding chair instead.

"So, what do you think?" Tyler asked, lowering himself into the armchair.

Of what? Paul wondered briefly. Obviously, he realized a moment later, Tyler wanted him to admire his arrangement of the room. Paul looked around. Where bookcases didn't hug the walls, plastic milk crates climbed from floor to ceiling, stuffed with an assortment of hardware:

Felix and adauctus

levels, machine belts in assorted sizes, rope, wrenches, power tools, measuring tapes, and jars and jars of hardware: nails, bolts, screws, keys, wall anchors. Tyler didn't seem to own a bureau, and his wardrobe and bedding filled half the shelves.

"You have a lot of boots," Paul noted, seizing on the first neutral remark that presented itself to his thoughts, and was surprised by the vehemence of Tyler's response.

"Most important piece of gear a construction worker owns! You don't have the right footwear, you'll get killed," he enthused, jumping to his feet. Crossing the floor he reached overhead for a tan work-boot, and carried it to where Paul was seated.

"This, for example," he explained, holding it out for inspection, "this is a piece of shit. Timberland. Look at that — the top is coming away from the sole. This used to be a serious work-boot but now it's just a fashion statement for the hip-hop kids. Anybody who's doing any kind of serious work? You can forget these."

"Now these..." He was on the move again, this time withdrawing a pair of boots similar in every way to the first but colored a darker brown. "These are better quality. But what I discovered, after I bought them was..."

Paul saw no way to avoid taking on the pair while Tyler moved to a neighboring bookcase.

"...that these are the best thing for construction work," he pronounced triumphantly, presenting a fourth boot for his visitor's perusal.

"Do you know what that is?" Tyler inquired, excitedly. Paul shrugged, hoping his ignorance would dampen his host's ardor. But Tyler was only warming to his subject.

"That's a hiking boot!" he exclaimed, turning it in his hand as he spoke.

"What's great about these is the support. Sometimes I'm climbing around like a monkey on the job. One wrong move and I'm a goner. A lot of the guys think the steel toe is the most important thing. Wrong. This..." He tapped the side of the boot, "...is the way to go. It gives you traction and support."

Paul nodded, then looked around for a place to unload the boots Tyler had rejected.

"Hey, you sure you don't want any wine?" Tyler asked, cheerfully

at home anywhere

expansive now, revived by the effort of enlightening his guest about his shoes and eager for continued company.

"No thanks. I've really got to get to bed. The restaurant was very busy and one of the waiters was out."

"Vodka then? C'mon, you need a drink! Lemme getcha' one!" Now Tyler was mildly bullying, in the same way that Paul remembered the real drinkers among his parents' friends could be.

"No, thanks, really…"

"I can't believe you're going to bed, man! How come you didn't stay in Manhattan? Things'd just be getting started! When I was a waiter in Dallas, the end of the shift was the beginning of the night for me. Time to hunt poontang! You can't beat those Texas honeys. I'll tell you what they oughta' do. They oughta' ship all the women in New York south for training. They give you such a hard time up here! You take my ex. I swear, she tried to kill me!"

Paul frowned, waiting for an explanation. This, at least, might prove interesting, he thought.

"See this?" Tyler said, pulling a baseball cap off the shelf behind his own chair. The silhouette of a naked woman adorned the crown. "I got one just like it in Texas when I first started working in construction. I thought it'd help me fit in with the rednecks."

"Did it work?" Paul asked, flatly. Apparently this topic would also revolve around apparel.

"Are you kidding? They loved it," Tyler replied, fondly remembering.

"But your girlfriend wasn't impressed," Paul prompted.

Now Tyler's face darkened. "I had to draw a line or she would have had me on a leash. At first I agreed not to wear it when we were out together with her daughter. So this one night we were going to a barbecue one of her yuppie friends was giving. I just grabbed the first hat that came to my hand and it happened to be the other one like this. I was going to put it back but then I thought, why should I? At the door she said, 'I thought we agreed?' So I compromised. Big mistake. I put the hat in my back pocket. Like this." He rose to demonstrate. "You think she appreciated it? All the way there she's giving me the cold shoulder, yapping away to the kid like I'm not even there.

"I was so sick of it by the time we got to the house that I made some excuse for not going in. About a block away I reached for the hat but

Felix and adauctus

it wasn't there. So I went back, retraced my steps. I looked everywhere, but I couldn't find it.

"By that time I was really angry. If she hadn't made such an issue out of the hat, I wouldn't have lost it. That's what's wrong with northerners. They just can't take a joke.

"I went home then, and by the time they got back I decided to forgive her. I even figured out how to score some points: I told her I threw the hat away because I realized how much she hated it.

"You think she appreciated that? She laughed at me. I swear, I wanted to push her. I've never hit a woman, but I was coming close. So I walked out. When I came back later I asked her why she laughed. She said the next guests to arrive after I left her off at the barbecue found the hat on the steps. They brought it in and asked who it belonged to. She was too embarrassed to claim it. No one else did, naturally, so they threw it out. And she let them. Can you believe that? Bitch. Lucky I found this one a few weeks later."

It was late, so Paul didn't point out that Tyler's own intention to lie in order to turn an accident to his advantage was no more honorable than his former girlfriend's failure to claim the embarrassing hat in front of her friends. Standing, he asked Tyler where he wanted the boots he was holding to go.

"Oh, don't worry about them. Just leave them on the floor. I'll get them later."

"Well, I guess I'll go then."

Paul had expected this announcement to remind his host of what it was that had prompted his invitation in the first place. But Tyler remained silent.

"Was there something in particular you wanted to ask me about?" he inquired, his bright waiter's voice concealing his impatience.

"What? Oh, no. I just thought you might like to see how I've settled in."

"Oh. Well, goodnight then," Paul said, turning toward the door. He knew he should be glad that Tyler seemed to be recovering from the upheaval of moving. But all he felt was resentment. He had lost ten minutes of meditation, prayer, and sleep in order to hear a lecture on work boots.

So when, just before entering the hall, he remembered Sonia's list,

83

at home anywhere

he stepped back inside.

"Oh, by the way, have you had a chance to do anything about the list Sonia left for you?"

"The list?"

"Of repairs."

"Oh, that. I'm going to try to get to that tomorrow."

"I think she's very serious about it."

Tyler went on as though he hadn't heard. "This whole moving thing just knocked me out. After two years of dealing with my spoiled girlfriend and her bratty daughter she kicks me out. Then coming in here and meeting you and Sonia and the dogs. It's been a lot."

Paul considered making the suggestion that Tyler might want to make a small start on one of the projects, to reassure Sonia of his good intentions. But he was too annoyed, and not just at Tyler's thoughtlessness in keeping him there to discuss his work-boots when he'd mentioned how tired he was several times. Sonia was also to blame, for putting him in the position of trying to preserve his own situation in her household while she brought in outsiders, and then for being so credulous, for liking Tyler so well so quickly. She ought to have known better than to accept the first candidate for her daughter's room, no matter whose recommendation had brought Tyler to her attention.

Since making mention of his former girlfriend, Tyler's frown hadn't lifted. He looked startled when Paul said goodnight again, as though it took him a moment to translate what he'd heard. "Oh, yeah — g'night," he said.

Paul worked the next day at SHARE. He tried to bring the same attitude of cordial professionalism to the soup-kitchen that made him so successful at the restaurant, but of course the clientele were very different. Seated around the tables at SHARE were about three dozen white and Hispanic men — either too pale or too ruddy, depending on their addiction — and dusty-looking black men with rheumy eyes. All dressed alike in cheap plaid shirts, sweat pants or dungarees, and brand-less sneakers. Paul's brothers, still living at home with his mother in the shabby frame house in La Frere, would fit right in.

As usual, only a handful of women had come to dine. To Paul's continuing surprise they didn't sit together, or exchange more than a

Felix and adauctus

few words, seeming to prefer the company of the men. Perhaps they felt less shame that way? He remembered that after his father left them, his mother had gone to greater pains to avoid their female neighbors than the male ones.

Sister Agatha, who had taught him to speak of the men and women as "clients," opened the door to the kitchen. "We're ready," she said. Paul and the other volunteers carried the steaming trays to the serving table. That morning one of the local restaurants had donated four chickens. Sister Agatha had cut them up and cooked them with tomato sauce and pasta. Canned string beans, courtesy of local school children, rounded out the meal. The beverages offered were cans of generic soda, coffee, and iced tea from a mix. Sister Agatha, her broad face still reddened from the heat in the kitchen, motioned Paul into place behind the chicken, which required the most expertise to serve in portions that appeared roughly equal. Then she led the assembly in a non-denominational prayer: "We give thanks to all who made this meal possible, amen."

After that the men and women lined up, the shy newcomers, the more relaxed regulars; a few even cheerful, joking. That capacity, to enjoy yourself under any circumstances, must be inborn, Paul thought, using a fork and the flat of a knife to lay the first serving of chicken on a client's plate. He didn't think that Tyler Landry would find much to smile about here.

He went right on to Mass after helping Sister Agatha clean up. Then to work. Leaving the subway early after all, he walked up Park Avenue instead of Madison, thereby avoiding temptation.

At home again he wasn't as disciplined, and went straight to the kitchen after greeting Mischa, who was alone. As expected, the list still lay in the bowl. His anxious satisfaction at finding it there was short-lived, quickly replaced by shame. He must be very bored to find Tyler's negligence amusing. Which meant he wasn't keeping spiritually active enough. He said a short prayer for forgiveness, but no sooner was the prayer complete when he wondered, with nervous anticipation, *what kind of scene will Sonia make when she returns?*

He heard Tyler turn in at the gate. If he went right to his room now, he

at home anywhere

could avoid a meeting, and any discussion of the troublesome list.

But that would be rude, considering that Tyler had taken Luke out for his nightly walk.

As he stood hesitating, the dogs approached the entrance to the house. Too late now, he thought, as Tyler turned the key in the lock and the metal door swung inward.

Tyler had stopped at Zen for take-out and urged Paul to join him.

"I ate at work," Paul muttered, stealing a glance at Tyler's feet, bare inside his Clark's slip-ons.

The phone rang. Tyler answered. "Sonia! Everything's great. I'm just about to dig into the Green Ocean Roll from Zen, so you know I'm happy!

"What's that? The list? No, I haven't seen it. Where did you say it was? Yeah, that's what Paul said, but you know I was moving things around in here the other day to do some cooking and I haven't seen it since. Maybe I knocked it off the counter! I'll look again. Hey, speaking of the devil, Paul's right here! You want to talk to him?"

Without giving Sonia time to answer, Tyler held out the phone.

"Hello?" Paul said, making his voice carefully neutral.

"How are things going?" asked Sonia.

"Fine."

"Good. Did you happen to hear what Tyler said? Can you help him look around for the list of repairs? It was in the blue bowl."

"Sure."

"It can't have gone far."

"I'll help him look."

"I should be home tomorrow at around noon."

"Great," said Paul. They hung up.

"She doesn't usually call," said Paul, glancing at the list and then back to Tyler. "I don't usually know this far in advance when she's coming home."

"That's lucky," said Tyler, using his wineglass to push the little bowl over the counter's edge. "Oops!" he said, as it crashed to the floor.

Paul startled. Then, keeping his dismay hidden, he said, "Her daughter made that."

"Aw, shucks. Then I guess she's going to be heartbroken," said Tyler.

86

Felix and adauctus

"Where's the broom?"

"In that closet. That still won't explain what happened to the list."

"This," said Tyler, sweeping the paper up with the shards of bowl, "is what happened to the list." As he spoke he withdrew a lighter from his pocket, then knelt and set the list alight.

From start to finish, the destruction of the bowl and its contents had only taken minutes. Now Paul knew why the first emotion people registered after witnessing violence was their surprise at the speed of its execution. "It happened so fast!" exclaimed the subway riders who'd watched a holdup unfold when they were interviewed on TV, as though that quality was the most noteworthy thing about the experience. Where their situation differed from his, Paul thought, was that here the perpetrator wasn't anonymous. Tyler had a key to the house, and Paul himself had invited him in, so that the classic onlooker's response — a sense of immunity from danger — was even more than usually mistaken. Up until now, he had assumed that Sonia would suffer the most serious consequences if Tyler failed to satisfy, because she owned the house. With the casual destruction of the blue bowl Paul's anticipation of whatever mild conflict might arise between those two over the issue of the repairs was replaced by dread. If he had to take sides, there was no doubt whose he would be on. As Sonia's ally, however, he became Tyler's enemy. And then Tyler might destroy — what? Paul owned nothing of value except Luke.

"The pieces are pretty large. I think it could be glued together," Paul offered, struggling to suppress the alarm swelling in his chest.

"Are you kidding? This piece of junk? She ought to thank me for getting rid of some of this clutter. You're the one who has to vacuum the place, don't you get sick of it?"

"It's not my home," said Paul, with a shrug.

"You live here, don't cha?"

"I rent a room. I suppose you could argue that the interior of my room is my home, but certainly nothing up here is."

"That's where you're wrong," said Tyler, tipping the dustpan into the garbage pail. "This place is as much yours as hers. And mine." Paul nearly laughed, but realized in time that Tyler was being serious. So he didn't scoff, just as at the restaurant he never demonstrated his personal feelings to a diner. He wasn't being paid for candor. The Code of the

87

at home anywhere

Kitchen served him well now. He made his face blank and said he was taking Luke out to get some bread.

The next day Paul returned to his room directly after breakfast, remaining there even when he heard Tyler go out. He wanted to wait until his housemate had a chance to explain himself to Sonia before making his own appearance.

He heard her greet the dogs on her arrival. Then she was on the telephone. A few minutes later he heard Tyler come in. "Hey! How was your trip!" Tyler exclaimed, heartily. He didn't hear what Sonia said next, or Tyler's reply.

Soon he heard Tyler call Teddy and cross the floor to the yard.

Climbing upstairs ten minutes later, he saw through the glass that Tyler had busied himself grooming the dog. Clouds of rust-brown fur drifted around the pair. After watching them for a moment, Paul turned into the living room, where Sonia sat facing the television. She glanced up as Paul entered.

"Paul. How are you?"

"Fine. I was just about to have some rice milk. Can I get you some?"

"No, thanks," Sonia replied, almost wistfully.

Moments later, standing at the kitchen counter as he drank, Paul watched Tyler, up on his knees, going at Teddy with the grooming comb. He put his whole body into the task, as if nothing else were as important.

After rinsing out his glass, Paul went to the patio door. "I'm going to walk the dogs," he said. "Do you want me to take Teddy?"

"I was going to take them!" Tyler protested, holding the brush in mid-air.

"I just thought, you've been taking them so much lately..."

"I don't mind!"

"I just don't want you to think, because you're new here, that you have to do extra..."

"It's no problem! I'll take 'em! I'm almost finished here; just give me a couple of minutes!"

"All right. Well, shall I close this, or are you...?"

"I'm coming in," Tyler said, scrambling to his feet.

Sonia had entered the kitchen in the meantime. As they approached she smiled, nervously.

"Now that you're both here, I wonder if either of you can tell me what happened to the blue bowl I left the list of repairs in? I just don't see it anywhere."

After a brief pause, Tyler explained that he'd found it that morning, broken, on the floor alongside the refrigerator.

"Oh! Did you save the pieces?" she asked.

"No, I didn't know you'd want them," Tyler went on. "I thought the best thing to do was get the pieces up quickly so the dogs didn't cut themselves."

"So it's gone?"

Tyler nodded. "The bag was full, so I took it right out to the curb."

Sonia's face fell. "My daughter made that bowl in kindergarten."

"I'm sorry," said Tyler, "I didn't know."

"Of course not. And you did have to think of the dogs. But you do have the list?"

"Uh, no. I'm sorry, but I don't remember seeing it. I may have swept it up with the broken pieces. I just don't recall coming across it."

Sonia sighed. "I'll make another one. Right now I'm going up to my room to rest. You can let the machine answer the phone if you don't want to take messages."

"Sure," said Tyler, sounding happier now that Sonia had accepted his story about the bowl. So Paul wasn't surprised when, after Sonia left, Tyler said Paul could take the dogs out after all.

Tyler found work the next day. When he arrived home at four-thirty Sonia moved quickly towards the remote control to lower the television volume. One glance at his face convinced her to wait to show him the new list of repairs, however. His pants and shirt were streaked with dirt. Red clay marked his hiking boots. Wordlessly, he carried a liquor store bag straight into the kitchen, where Paul was preparing to rinse some beans, and poured himself a vodka and orange juice.

"I'll be out of here in a few minutes," said Paul.

"Take your time," Tyler replied, gruffly. A moment later, when he had downed a few more gulps of his drink, he sighed and set the glass down. "That's better. I've been thinking about that drink since noon! You should see the goons I'm working with. The way they talk. 'Pick it up! What are you afraid of?! It's not shit!' It's either gangsters, or Jamaicans. They may have better manners, but you can't understand a word they say. They all own their own houses though. The foreman on this job is a Jamaican. He's doing better than me. Yep. That's my country. Don't have enough work for the natives? Bring in some foreigners!"

As Paul set the beans onto the stove, Sonia appeared. Apparently she had planned to make an announcement of some kind, but caught the last part of Tyler's speech and stood watching him silently, a tentative smile on her face.

"I'm making vegetarian chili," said Paul, to break the tension. "It's going to have red peppers and corn in it. There's going to be plenty, so please help yourself if I'm not here," he went on, smartly, as he might describe the specials at the restaurant.

"That sounds wonderful," said Sonia, without conviction, seeming to want to conserve her energies for her real mission. "Hello, Tyler. You seemed upset when you came in, so I wanted to give you a few minutes to unwind," she began.

"Upset? Me? I'm not upset," he said, bitterly. "Just because I have to take orders from a bunch of illiterates all day long? What makes you think that would upset me!"

Still smiling, Sonia furrowed her brows, as though debating whether to address his complaints or ignore them. After a moment she plunged in. "Well, I just wanted to let you know that I made another list of repairs. It's behind you, on the refrigerator," she said, gesturing towards the sheet of paper pinned up behind a magnet.

Lifting his drink to his lips Tyler said, "Oh yeah. I see it. Well, great."

"If there's anything you don't understand, please ask," she said.

"You bet," he replied.

"I'm going out now, just for a few hours."

"I probably won't be here when you get back," Paul warned.

"Well — have a good shift!" she said, weakly, and then she left them, trying not to hurry.

They heard her greet a neighbor outside the house. A moment later Tyler placed his glass into the sink. "Time for a nap," he said, stretching luxuriantly.

"Shall I take the dogs out?"

"Maybe Mischa. I'll take the others to the park when I get up."

Felix and adauctus

"Great. Thanks."

"No problema," Tyler said, easily, rubbing his chest with his long, slender fingers. Paul marveled at how swiftly his mood had changed. All the tension had left his body. It was as though Tyler thought he had permanently evaded responsibility for making the repairs on the list, and not just effected a temporary postponement.

Two days later, the list still lay pinned to the refrigerator. This time, Sonia didn't give Tyler the opportunity to take those few gulps of vodka when he arrived home before following him into the kitchen.

"Tyler, I wonder if I could speak with you."

"Sure. Fire away," he said, brusquely, removing the vodka from the freezer, fishing inside the refrigerator for the juice.

"Well, I wondered if this would be a good time to walk through the repairs that you agreed to do."

"Good a time as any. I've been ordered around all day, I guess I should be used to it by this time!"

Paul, stirring a curry sauce, could almost feel Sonia stiffen.

"I know we discussed them once already, but it's been a while since then and I thought it would be a good idea for both of us to refresh our memory of just what needs to be done."

"No problem. Have a drink first," he replied, pushing the vodka towards her. "Paul, make yourself useful. Get Sonia here a glass."

"No thank you," she said, curtly.

"You sure?" said Tyler, falsely convivial. "Aw, c'mon, have a drink! Things may go better with coke, but they REALLY go better with vodka!"

"No, thank you. It's really too early for me."

"You wouldn't last long in Dallas," he replied. Sonia managed an uneasy smile.

Tyler took his time, drinking. Ignoring Sonia, he directed all his subsequent remarks at Paul, admiring the sauce and teasing him about his affinity for cooking. At last, draining off his glass, he motioned to Sonia and said, "Lead on."

She nodded toward the refrigerator. "Don't you think you should bring the list?"

"The list. Right! Can't forget the list!" he exclaimed, sardonically. Returning to the refrigerator he slid the magnet to one side and lifted up the paper behind it.

They started in the backyard, where Sonia pointed out the fire escape. Paul took the potatoes out of the steamer and added them to the spices in the pan, glancing over his shoulder from time to time to follow the progress the other two made. They had moved towards the middle of the yard, where Sonia was obviously pointing out the paving stones that needed replacement. Tyler stood alongside, arms folded, nodding. Not overjoyed, but resigned to following Sonia around, and she appeared greatly reassured.

Paul had to leave before they came inside. For the first time in days he felt optimistic that things between them might work out. He wouldn't have to choose sides, or worse: find someplace else to live when Sonia blamed him for introducing her to Tyler.

His optimism was short-lived.

Sonia went away again, this time for just two days.

Tyler was out when she returned. After giving Paul a perfunctory greeting, she went straight into the yard.

Returning a moment later, having quickly determined that no progress had been made on the repairs, she stood opposite him across the counter and asked, wearily, "Has Tyler been home much?"

"The same as before," said Paul.

"Before when he was working or before that, when he wasn't?"

"He's been working. I assume. He's already gone when I get up in the morning. He gets home at about 4:30 every afternoon. Well, on the weekdays."

Sonia looked exasperated. "Has he said anything to you about why he hasn't started the work? Is he sick or something? Does he need supplies? He told me that he had everything he needed."

"He hasn't said anything to me. He's been going to work every day, so I don't think he's sick…"

They heard the gate swing open. *Quick*, thought Paul, irrationally; *hide!*

Sonia shook her head from side to side and pressed her lips together. "I just don't understand," she said, regretfully.

"Hey!" Tyler cried, entering the living room. Like conspirators, Paul and Sonia moved apart. "I got a can of those stuffed grape leaves in

Felix and adauctus

here somewhere," Tyler announced, appearing in the kitchen a moment later, his arms laden with shopping bags from the local supermarket.

"Ever had these? Here, open that, why don't cha?" Tyler crowed, tossing a can towards Paul once he had deposited the bags on the counter.

"No thanks," Paul demurred, catching the can and setting it down alongside the other groceries. "Not for me. Not right now," he said. "Sonia?"

"No thanks."

"Well, I want some," said Tyler, with feigned petulance. After holding the can under the electric opener, he grabbed a fork from the drainer and speared one of the fragrant little packets of rice.

"Mmmm. That's tasty. Sure you don't want some? Help yourself!"

"I'm really not hungry," Sonia said, quickly, "But there is something I'd like to discuss with you, Tyler."

A grain of oily rice sat alongside Tyler's mouth. "Oh?"

"I think you can probably guess what it is."

"If you'll excuse me, I need to get ready for Mass," Paul interrupted, but Sonia remained in the doorway, seeming not to hear.

Tyler shrugged. "No, I can't," he said, abandoning the sham conviviality that had so far marked his voice. "So I guess you're going to have to tell me." Jamming the fork into the can, he set it down on the counter and folded his arms.

"That's a little hard to believe, Tyler. But all right," she said, reasonably. "Your flyer said that you were a handyman and that you were willing to exchange some of your skills for a place to live. When you moved in it was with the understanding that you would undertake some repair projects here. I think I made it very clear that that was part of the bargain. Paul here can vouch for that, can't you?"

"Sure," said Paul, blandly. *If only he had left the kitchen a little earlier!* Then again, Sonia might have waited until he was present before confronting Tyler.

"Well of course he's going to agree with you," Tyler scoffed. "You may run his life, but you don't run mine!"

Sonia seemed startled by the sudden shift of topic. And by Tyler's altered features. From the generous, smiling fellow urging them to share his grape leaves, he'd become sullen, and slightly menacing.

"What is that supposed to mean?" said Sonia.

"For what I'm paying for that room up there, I shouldn't have to do anything extra! You may have him fooled into thinking he's got some kind of great deal here, cleaning up after your mess and looking after your dogs! But you can't fool me. I thought you'd get the hint about the god-damned list, but I guess you're not as smart as you think you are!"

"So you don't intend to do the work."

"You got that right."

"Then the terms of our agreement aren't being met."

Tyler shrugged, petulantly.

"I just want to make sure I understand you," Sonia replied calmly. Her complacency apparently confused Tyler, and he continued to argue his case.

"You've got a nice little racket running here, but you can count me out," he said, and then, driving home his point: "You're double-dipping, that's what you're doing, expecting me to pay rent and work!"

Removing the fork from the can he dropped it into the sink and placed the can of grape leaves into the refrigerator. Then he moved towards Sonia, who held her ground until the very last minute before stepping aside to let Tyler pass.

Tyler climbed the stairs. At the top he whistled for Teddy, who followed him up.

When they heard the door close Sonia stepped closer to Paul, lowering her voice before speaking. "Do you think he'd do anything?"

"What do you mean?" said Paul.

"Get violent. Do you think I should be worried?"

"Oh no. I mean, he lived with that woman and her daughter," Paul offered, with a confidence he didn't feel.

"But they broke up."

"You talked to her, though."

"Maybe she lied, to get rid of him faster."

"I suppose that's possible, but — I don't think so," Paul finally brought out, feebly. "I mean, I think he's somewhat immature, but not — violent."

Sonia silently nodded. Paul didn't think he'd convinced her. He hadn't convinced himself. By the time he left the kitchen a few minutes later, she had passed into the living room and resumed watching television. One arm lay folded over her chest. With the other she unconsciously stroked her neck. Paul descended the steps to his room.

Felix and adauctus

After that they all stayed more in their rooms, uneasily navigating the common areas of the house. Sonia visibly tensed whenever her path crossed Tyler's. But he was never anywhere long, and didn't say much even to Paul.

Two nights after the confrontation over the grape leaves, Sonia called Paul into her room as he started towards the shower. It was after midnight. She had waited up to let him know that she had to go away again, to Hudson, where she was leading a workshop for adult survivors of dysfunctional families. This time she wanted him to have her telephone number at the conference center there so he could let her know immediately if anything happened while she was gone.

"She here?" Tyler had arrived home.

"No."

"Good. Stupid bitch. She may have had kids, but I'm telling you, she's a carpet-muncher if I ever saw one."

"She's what?"

"A carpet-muncher! You never heard that expression? She's gay!"

"Oh."

"I'm telling you, they have it in for men. Even more so than other women. They'd all work us into the grave if they could, but with dykes it's a religion. Only I don't intend to let her."

"She's just upset," Paul said. Then, provoked by Tyler's remarks about lesbians, he added, stoutly, "You did agree to do the work."

But the effort was futile; Tyler looked pleased! "I did, didn't I? Too bad. Life's rough sometimes. It certainly is for me. Why shouldn't she get a taste of what I go through every day?"

"Did you ever intend to do the work?"

"Oh yeah. When I first met her, I did. But once I figured out her game, I decided. She's not getting away with it. Not with me."

"What is her 'game'?"

"Look at the way she's got you trained! You clean for her, you cook for her…"

"I cook because I enjoy it. It's not one of my official duties."

"And how often does she return the favor?"

"Often enough." Not, he realized, as often as she shared his food.

"And you do all that vacuuming. I mean, I could see if you didn't pay any rent. But you do. And she's got you doing all this other shit."

"My rent is very low, though. Especially for this neighborhood. I wouldn't be able to live in this area if I had to pay market rent."

"That's not the point! You could get a share in an apartment for probably not much more than you're paying here. At least you'd have your freedom. And your dignity. You're nothing but a houseboy, here. Don't you have any pride?"

"I don't feel that what Sonia asks me to do is excessive. And I have more freedom this way."

"How do you figure that?"

"Since I don't have to spend as much on where I live, I don't have to work as many hours. So I can spend some time doing the things I really care about."

"Like what? Going to Mass? You could still do that if you lived somewhere else."

"Probably not every day. And I wouldn't be able to volunteer at SHARE."

"That's that place for the homeless? Meanwhile you're nearly homeless yourself. You think that carpet-muncher cares about you? Take my word for it, if she could find some dyke to do her dirty work, you'd be out of here in no time!"

Until today Paul had succeeded in restraining himself from an open display of amusement at Tyler's pronouncements. Now, however — perhaps because the atmosphere had been so tense lately — Tyler's description of lesbian conspiracy made him laugh aloud. And once started he couldn't seem to stop.

"Go ahead and laugh," Tyler scowled. "Everyone else does. I thought you were my friend. I don't know why."

"I'm sorry. You just — you sound so serious…!"

"I am serious! You think I like to see that double-dipper taking advantage of you? I wish somebody cared as much about me! I wish I had somebody to give me advice!"

Paul worked to control himself, but every time he glanced at Tyler's face, twisted with self-pity, he broke down. "I'm sorry," he giggled, "I don't know why this is striking me so funny…!"

"And I don't know why I'm wasting my breath. You obviously don't appreciate it," Tyler muttered, and left the room.

Felix and adauctus

Paul continued cooking. Bursts of laughter escaped his lips and tears filled his eyes as he remembered Tyler's ravings. The man was crazy. Completely paranoid. How would Sonia get rid of him? Paul didn't see how she could. They were stuck!

When he had poured the soup into three containers, marking two for the freezer and placing one in the lower part of the refrigerator, he started towards the broom closet to get the vacuum cleaner. He liked to do the first floor and the stairs every other day. He had arrived at the schedule, not Sonia. She had simply asked him to do his best to keep the dog hair under control.

At the closet, hand on the knob, he hesitated. She wasn't here. She wouldn't know if he had skipped a day or not. And he did pay rent.

His hand fell to his side. Then he brought it to rest on the doorknob again. His arrangement with Sonia was in many ways ideal. The arguments he'd made to Tyler were all true: the rent was way below market rates, even for a share. He did have time for the things that were important to him. He didn't feel that she was taking advantage of him. Definitely not.

He did wish she'd thought of offering him Emma's room, however.

"Luke!" he called, walking to the front of the house. "Come! Come here, Luke!"

He would take Luke to the park alone, leaving the other dogs until later.

He hadn't done that in ages.

This time when Sonia returned she wasn't alone. Paul recognized her companion. Small and fair, with a thin face, Polly wore tie-dyed clothing that was faded with wear. They'd been introduced a few months earlier, when Polly returned with Sonia from a weekend retreat at an ashram in upstate New York and stayed overnight in Park Slope before going on to her own apartment in Manhattan. After greetings were exchanged, the women pulled chairs up to the table in the dining room. Paul had just served them a pot of tea when Tyler surprised them by entering the room from the garden.

"Paul," he said, pointedly ignoring the women.

"Hello, Tyler. Sonia's here. And this is Polly."

"Hi," Tyler muttered, glowering.

"Tyler, we need to discuss the terms of your residence here," Sonia began. "Unless, of course, you've started the work we agreed upon?"

Polly gave a nervous cough. Tyler stared at her. She smiled, apologetically.

"I don't think there's anything to discuss. I pay my rent," he said, brusquely.

"But that wasn't what we agreed upon when I invited you to live here," Sonia replied, with studied reasonableness. "I also wonder if you can explain why there's so much furniture in your room."

"You've been in my room?"

"No. I was on the stoop today. I went out to pick up some menus. I noticed the furniture through the window."

After a brief pause, Tyler shrugged. "So what? Things change. I'm here now. I pay my rent," he repeated, doggedly.

"But we didn't discuss the changes. You made them without consulting me."

"If you ask me, people do too much discussing. There's nothing to discuss. You tried to take advantage of me and I'm not going to let you do that."

Polly spoke. "Won't you sit down?"

"Yes, please," said Sonia. "Paul, would you bring us another mug please?"

"I don't want anything. And I don't want to sit down. I'm going upstairs."

Sonia stood up, blocking his path. Polly stood up too.

"Tyler, I want you to leave my home. As soon as possible. You have one week to find somewhere else to stay."

Clearly, Tyler hadn't expected her ultimatum, but the shock made him look only slightly less threatening, despite the smile he managed to work up.

"What! I can't believe you're making such a big deal out of this," he said, feigning wounded surprise. "I'm a good tenant! I pay my rent, don't I? I'm clean, aren't I? You could hire somebody to do those jobs! Easy! It wouldn't even cost you that much. Why would you want to get rid of somebody who pays the rent?"

"Because you didn't live up to your part of the agreement," Sonia said, curtly. Visibly confident now with Tyler in retreat she went on: "If

Felix and adauctus

you had made a good faith effort to fulfill your promises, and found the work was more than you expected, we could have talked it over and come to some arrangement. But I don't think you ever had any intention of doing the work. I think you thought you could just agree to everything and then move in here and do whatever you wanted. But you can't. I don't feel that I can trust you, so I'm giving you notice. You have one week to find somewhere else to live."

Sonia and Tyler stared at each other. Polly stared at Sonia; probably, Paul guessed, because she was afraid to stare at Tyler. Looking on from behind the counter, Paul wondered who would be the first to give way: stocky Sonia in silver and black, with wispy, tie-dyed Polly as back-up; or Tyler, who'd definitely lost some of his starch.

Finally Tyler shifted and brought a hand to his hip. "A week. That's not much time."

"That's what you have."

"I'm going to need more time. That's only fair. I have paid my rent, haven't I? I think you owe me that much."

"You're paid up to the end of next week."

"Hey, but you know how tough it is in this neighborhood. Do you think I even would have come in here if I could have found somewhere else to live? I'm going to need more time."

"All right. Two weeks. But that's all."

"If you're sure that's what you want..." he began, still hoping to induce Sonia to grant a reprieve. Polly sank into her chair, but Sonia, unmoved, remained standing as he brushed past her. Then she too sat down. The women looked at each other. Polly widened her eyes. "That wasn't as..." she began, but Tyler had spent only seconds in his room, and was again descending the stairs, with Teddy in tow. They didn't resume speaking until certain he had left the house.

"He didn't lock the door," said Sonia.

"I'll get it," said Paul, relieved that so far neither Tyler nor Sonia had seemed to recall the role he'd played in bringing them together.

He returned to the women's weak laughter. "He is tall. You were right about that!" Polly said, "I can see now why you'd be frightened."

"The most frightening thing is how illogical he is. It's like, if one tactic doesn't work, he just switches gears. Doesn't he realize other people are keeping track?" Sonia sighed. "He seems so pathetic now. But that's

at home anywhere

because you're both here. Well, I guess I've learned my lesson. No more sharing with single men."

Polly looked at Paul. "I'm sure you mean 'present company excepted', of course," she said, smiling nervously.

Sonia laughed. "Oh, Paul. Paul's a different matter entirely."

"I'm going to take the dogs out now," he said.

"Good," said Sonia. "Enjoy yourselves. I'm going to order in from Zen. Finish off anything that interests you when you get back."

It was early enough in the springtime that Paul was surprised each evening when he left the house and found it still light. It gave the day a sense of unreality, not entirely welcome, considering the scene that had just taken place. He started off briskly for the park, hoping the exercise would set him at ease.

Halfway across Seventh Avenue he saw Tyler Landry exiting the liquor store with a bag under his arm. Averting his eyes, Paul quickened his pace. But Tyler had already seen him.

"Hey Paul!"

Paul got to the other side before stopping, and ordered the dogs to sit. Tyler loped up, Teddy at his side. "They still in the house?" he asked.

"Sonia and Polly? They were when I left. They were ordering take-out."

Tyler nodded. "Where you goin'?" he asked, hollowly.

"Park," he replied, though he thought his destination should be obvious. But the location didn't seem to register with Tyler.

"Think I should go back?" he asked.

"I'm sure Sonia understands that you've got to stay there while you're looking for another place," Paul replied, sensibly. Tyler nodded, but made no move to start away, as if unwilling to leave a friendly voice.

"Well, I'd better go," said Paul, rousing the dogs, relieved when Tyler didn't ask to accompany them. Sonia was right about one thing: Tyler did now seem pathetic. But how could he be surprised at her decision? He had said he would do the repairs. She had reason to be upset with him, even without knowing what really became of the blue bowl. So Tyler was certainly the primary architect of his own misfortune. Yet his sermons on the subject of Sonia Fisher were not without effect. Previously Paul had

Felix and adauctus

considered her a kind of patron. At their first interview she explained that her healing practice was based on Eastern spiritual principals. The fact encouraged him to share his plans for the priesthood, and she had seemed genuinely pleased that the rental arrangement she was offering would facilitate that pursuit. Once Tyler introduced the notion that theirs might not be as equitable an arrangement as he had thought, Paul found himself reexamining his assumptions. For several weeks after he'd moved in, Sonia had continued to feed and walk the dogs. But now he couldn't remember when she had last done so.

And the room he lived in! Nearly windowless, the only outside light coming from the skylight exit to the yard at the rear of the house. For which he paid two hundred dollars a month.

But that included heat and electricity. He got few calls; Sonia paid the entire phone bill in return for his taking down her messages. A bargain, in this neighborhood. A safe neighborhood generally, and famously tolerant of homosexuals, who were always targets of violence, whether or not they were sexually active.

Paul had reached the top of the slope. The park lay directly ahead.

Entering at Third Street he started south, nodding to the other dog walkers he met along the way while the pets made their closer greetings. He went almost as far as Eighth Street before turning back. People coursed around the statue of Lafayette as they entered and left the park. Somehow he didn't want to join them.

Just shy of where he had come in he stopped again, this time leaning against the perimeter wall while the dogs circled in the bushes behind him, panting and snuffling in the fallen leaves. Way down the slope the sun had just set. At the bottom the houses would be faced with orange light, but up here the limestone buildings opposite the park looked blue. Where would he go, if he had to move? The task of finding housing in New York was always harrowing. So why did he suddenly feel elated?

For the next few days, Sonia remained in her room, except for brief periods following Tyler's morning departure, and again after he took his shower and retired to his room for the night. Twice daily she called Paul in to her office to ask for reports of Tyler's movements. Was he making any progress towards finding a new place? Had he expressed anything about his feelings toward her?

at home anywhere

Paul tried to reassure her but couldn't provide much concrete evidence of how Tyler's housing search was going. He had taken messages from a few realtors. But so far Tyler hadn't said whether anything had come of these.

The state of affairs changed the following day.

"I was wonderin' when you were going to get up!" Tyler hailed him from the oak table when Paul came upstairs for breakfast. "I made some grits. Help yourself!"

"No thanks. They're not very nutritious, you know," he said, thinking how like grits Tyler actually was: visually appealing but short on substance.

"Well pour out some coffee then! It's fresh! I have a business proposition for you!"

He had seen Tyler shy, when he first presented himself for approval as a member of Sonia's household. Then sly, when he was making up a story about what happened to the bowl. Then mean, when he was talking about Sonia and her pressumed sexual orientation. But Paul hadn't seen Tyler this cheerful in a very long time, so decided not to bother making the reminder that he never drank coffee. After putting water on to boil for tea he joined Tyler at the table.

"So, what's the proposition?" he asked, evenly.

"Last night I had a great idea. We should get an apartment together!"

Paul acted thoughtful, his mind racing. In fact it was a terrible idea, but he couldn't say that outright.

"We get along," Tyler went on, "The dogs get along. It'd be perfect! Just think: no more tiles to dry after taking a shower. You can come and go as you please without having to notify that carpet-muncher. Whaddya' think?!"

"I'm...I'm pretty happy here."

"Happy!? How can you be happy being a cabin boy? You're at her beck and call; I've heard you telling her where you're going and when you'll be back and to go on and help herself to your food..."

"All common courtesy. I tell you when I'm going out, if you're around. Oh! — there's the water for my tea."

Paul excused himself to pour boiling water over a red zinger bag. Tyler meanwhile proceeded to describe an apartment he'd seen on First Street the day before. It was right across from the local elementary school,

102

Felix and adauctus

in one of those cooperative buildings where they hadn't been able to sell all the apartments.

"...Place has all new construction: new kitchen, new bathroom. It's perfect for a share, it's huge..."

"How much is the rent?" Paul asked, with what he hoped was the right combination of disinterested curiosity.

"Twelve hundred."

He took a gulp of the hot, sweet tea. "Let's see, that'd be — six hundred dollars a month for each of us. I only pay two hundred here. That's quite a jump."

"So we'll get another roommate. The place is big enough! At least say you'll come to see it with me. C'mon, I've been doing this whole thing on my own. Just say you'll take a look at it. I told the realtor I'd be bringing someone with me. I told her I'd be sharing the place, so she'd know the rent wouldn't be a problem. You have to come. You owe me that much!"

Actually, thought Paul, he didn't see how he owed Tyler anything at all.

Then he remembered their first meeting at the food co-op. If Paul hadn't been so eager to protect his own place in Sonia's house, Tyler would never have moved in with them. He might have found a better situation, and almost certainly would not be looking for housing again so soon. "All right," he said, finally, "I'll come."

Paul couldn't tell if the agent, a middle-aged woman with a Scandinavian accent, thought Tyler was a serious prospect or not. Tyler wasn't helping his own case. For one thing, he seemed very anxious, shifting from foot to foot, looking away from Mrs. Nilson whenever she spoke. In fact, once she realized what little information she would get out of Tyler, she directed all her questions to Paul.

"Tyler tells me that you are sharing a place together at present," she said, cheerfully.

"Yes, that's right," said Paul. He had remained standing just inside the apartment entrance, visually following Tyler's progress through the rooms. Her query reminded him that he was supposed to appear to be looking with Tyler, so he marched suddenly into the kitchen and began opening cabinet doors.

103

at home anywhere

"May I ask what rent you are currently paying?" Mrs. Nilson inquired, coming in after him.

"Oh, we split everything fifty-fifty," he said, quickly leaving the room.

Tyler was standing in the bathroom, looking up at the skylight. "Have you seen enough?" Paul murmured.

Tyler looked confused. "What?"

"Do you need to see any more?"

"No. No, I'm all set."

Outside the building Mrs. Nilson handed out business cards. "I'm sure you need some time to discuss the apartment," she said. "So I'll give you both one of these and that way you can call me if you decide that you are interested."

"Oh, I am interested," Tyler exclaimed, suddenly alert, even agitated: "I told you that on the phone! I'm very interested!"

Mrs. Nilson looked at Paul. "Well, I'm sure that Paul here might want to discuss it with you, since he has just seen it," she said, doubtfully.

"If he doesn't want to come, I'll get someone else. I know a lot of people, it won't be hard for me to find someone," Tyler said.

Mrs. Nilson frowned. "As I said earlier, this owner really isn't interested in renting to unrelated people…"

"We're not related!" Tyler frantically protested, "I never said we were related!"

"Well, not by blood, but you did say that you have been sharing an apartment for some time," she demurred.

"Oh, yeah, we do," Tyler said, cagily, seeing where he'd made his error and attempting to limit the damage. "But I'd never force him to go with me if I took a new place and he decided that he didn't want to come."

Casting Paul a sympathetic glance, Ms. Nilson spoke. "Well, gentlemen!" she said, briskly, abandoning the effort to pin down the precise nature of their relationship; "You have my card! Call me if you come to any decision." With a little wave, she strode to her car and climbed in.

"So, what did you think?" Tyler asked, expanding in her absence. "It's great, isn't it? You could get out of that basement. See some daylight once in a while!"

Felix and adauctus

"I see daylight at Sonia's."

"You'd see more. And you'd be out from under her thumb."

"Tyler, I just can't afford it. Anyway, as you said upstairs, you'll have no trouble finding someone else to share with…"

"Oh, I get it. You're upset because it sounded like I was abandoning you. I'm sorry. I want you to come in with me. I really do! You're my first choice, man. Really!"

"I'm flattered," Paul lied, wearily. "But seriously, Tyler, I'm going to stay at Sonia's. I told you that before I left and nothing I saw or heard here changed my mind."

Tyler stared at him as he spoke, his features slackening, becoming dull and hostile. He shrugged. "Suit yourself," he said, flatly, and stalked away.

Paul went directly to work after that. Ordinarily his reflection in the windows of the shops along Madison Avenue reassured him of his role in the life of the city. The part he played in the tableau created nightly at Les Trois Oiseaux seemed to him to make a fitting complement to his work at SHARE. Tonight, however, his place seemed tenuous everywhere. In this part of town he was just someone from the outer boroughs on a day pass. In Park Slope he was as little attached to the market-rate-apartment half of the world as Tyler. And he wasn't all that indispensable at SHARE. None of the clients had warmed to him, as they did to the other volunteers. Sometimes when he overheard them talking, they reminded him of Tyler, by turns boastful and beaten. He'd thought he was doing so much good working there, but it was easy charity. Helping Tyler would have cost much more, and he hadn't found it in his heart to do so.

These thoughts so consumed his attention that he didn't realize he had walked past the Egoiste shoe store until he was a block from the restaurant.

Home from work, Paul found a note from Sonia: "Please see me before you go to bed."

"It's locked," she cried, answering his knock, "Who is it?"

"Paul," he replied, surprised and troubled by the fear in her voice. Had Tyler become violent after all? When she opened the door, he saw that her face was tear-stained.

"Come in," she said.

at home anywhere

"Are you all right?"

"Physically, yes," she said, directing him into a velvet chair at the foot of the bed. "I can't say the same for my emotional state. Please sit down."

She lowered herself into an armchair alongside her desk, clearing her throat before speaking. "I don't know where to begin. I'm so — disheartened. Tyler was one thing. But I really thought I could trust you. It's quite a shock to learn just how poor a judge of character I am."

"What do you mean?"

"A realtor called earlier this evening. A Mrs. Nilson. She left a message that said she showed you an apartment today."

"Oh, that," he said, smiling as he recalled Mrs. Nilson's confusion. "Tyler asked me to go with him to look at a place. Apparently he told the agent that he had a roommate so she'd consider him a better prospect financially. I'm sorry. He seemed so desperate to have me go and I thought it might help him to find another place more quickly."

Sonia nodded, wanly, staring at him the way teachers did in grade school when, already convinced of your guilt, they attempted to shame you into a morally strengthening confession. "Well, that sounds reasonable," she admitted, finally. "But if that's the case, then I wonder why she said she'd be happy to show you more apartments if you decided not to go with Tyler."

He giggled. He couldn't help it. "I'm sorry — I know I shouldn't laugh. But you know Tyler and his stories! He tells such whoppers! Like today. After we looked at the apartment, Mrs. Nilson said that we probably needed time to talk before deciding if we were interested in the place. Tyler thought she was giving him the brush-off, so he panicked. He told her that if I didn't like the apartment, he'd find another roommate. She seemed kind of shocked that he would dump me right in front of a stranger when apparently he'd built up this whole story about what close friends we were! I guess she felt sorry for me, and that's why she left that message."

Sonia continued to gaze at him searchingly.

"Sonia, I swear I have no intention of looking for another apartment," he said, solemnly. "I am perfectly contented here. I consider this my home."

Finally her face softened. Just as he realized that in fact he would not stay, she smiled.

Felix and adauctus

Outside her room he took a moment to compose himself. Now he must be doubly careful. Until he had somewhere else to go, Sonia couldn't know his mind, but neither could Tyler. He certainly had no intention of moving in with him.

That Thursday Tyler found a place, an illegal storefront apartment not far from the Prospect Expressway. On Saturday he moved out. The whole process went very quickly; Paul left for the park with the dogs at the start of the proceedings, and by the time he had returned a little more than two hours later, Tyler was tying the final bookcase atop the car.

"Come over later," he said, taking Teddy's leash. "The dogs can see each other."

"I can't," Paul said, "I have Mass."

"You can miss Mass this once! C'mon! I want to show you my new place!"

"It's really impossible today, Tyler," Paul said firmly.

When Paul didn't relent, Tyler changed the subject: "How was the park? Anybody we know up there?"

"I didn't see anyone. Think you'll make it tomorrow morning?"

"What? Oh, yeah! Yeah, I'll be there," Tyler said, brightening at the prospect of keeping touch with at least one aspect of what was rapidly becoming his old life. "What time are you going up?"

"Seven, seven-thirty."

"I'll be there. Wait for me, you hear?"

"I will."

Tyler opened the front door and called Teddy into the car. Then he folded himself inside. When his long-fingered hand reached out to adjust the mirror, Paul thought how much he looked like a cartoon man, jammed inside an impossibly tiny vehicle, and wondered how Tyler could ever have reminded him of the boys at home, for whom everything in the world — shirts and coats and cars and shoes — seemed tailored.

Paul expected to feel relief once Tyler was gone, but found to his surprise that he missed him. Well, perhaps that wasn't it exactly. Only, his own discontent didn't ebb, and he no longer had Tyler as a distraction.

Sonia emerged from self-exile. She was like someone newly back from a hospital stay, happy just to be moving again among familiar

107

things. Paul was glad for her, but her joy made his own dissatisfaction more acute. She had lost something of sentimental value, and suffered a few days of uncertainty. But she had her speaking tours and her daughters and this house. He reminded himself of the periods of uncertainty many of the saints reported, when they doubted the path they had chosen. And of the vows of poverty he would someday take. But his readiness was no consolation.

That week at the food collective, he was assigned to train a new member. Adrien Rosen wore a Tibetan vest and Birkenstock sandals, which, when Paul admired them, he boasted had come from the Hadassah Thrift Shop on Flatbush Avenue and cost next to nothing.

Unfortunately, Adrien's gift for bagging bargains at the thrift shop didn't translate into getting raisins packaged very efficiently. Paul didn't recall just how long it had taken him to become proficient at the task, but he'd never seen anyone as slow as Adrien, whose plastic gloves were still sticking to the raisins after nearly an hour on the job.

"Couldn't I pay you to do this for me?" Adrien asked, plaintively. Giddy with failure, he held out his hands when Paul proffered a new pair of gloves. And Paul, responding automatically, moved closer and began to roll the gloves over Adrien's hands, which were dry and delicate, the fingers slightly webbed; not at all like Tyler's.

"Against co-op rules," he replied, suddenly releasing Adrien's hands before the gloves were fully on, and returning to his side of the table. Then, as Adrien continued to struggle, he relented. "But maybe I can convince the board to pay you *not* to. Meanwhile, why don't you start weighing?"

"Thank you," Adrien said, peeling off the gloves. He looked both older and younger than his twenty-six years. His features were small and soft but his black hair, tied back in a ponytail, was already threaded with grey. He wore thick blue socks under his sandals, so Paul couldn't tell what his feet were like. He worked as a floor clerk at the stock exchange and had come to the food collective right from work. He had just moved from his parent's home in Flatbush to an apartment on Dean Street. Paul said that he might soon need to find another place to live, and Adrien replied that he was about to start looking for a roommate to share expenses with.

Felix and adauctus

When he heard how reasonable the rent would be, Paul expressed cautious interest, and Adrien said that he would leave his keys with the landlady the next day so Paul could take a look at the place.

The apartment was on the second floor of a run-down building near Flatbush Avenue. The landlady was very elderly, and seemed somewhat confused when Paul arrived to ask for the keys. Finally he gave up trying to explain his errand, and walked away. He had reached the corner when it started to rain and by the time he got back to Sonia's he was thoroughly wet. The dogs stirred only briefly, returning to their places at his command. Sonia was out. The light on her answering machine was blinking, but Paul did not move to write down her calls. Instead he sat at the dining room table and looked out at the dripping garden.

Then suddenly he got to his feet, and hurried to the telephone to call Adrien to let him know he wanted the room.

Paul made a few attempts at trying to convince Sonia that he wasn't leaving her to join Tyler. He even offered to bring Adrien around one afternoon so they could meet, but Sonia had taken to her room, as she had during Tyler's last days. Polly was present when he moved out, as inappropriately deferential to her friend's enemies as ever.

He told Sister Agatha and the restaurant manager that he was moving and would miss a couple of days at SHARE and Les Trois Oiseaux. He didn't make it to Mass on Friday, moving day. Adrien had a lot of books and they spent all day shifting bookcases around to empty a room for Paul. At first Paul noticed the titles — many of the books were about Asian history and culture, including a whole shelf of volumes on Tibet. But after a while he didn't bother reading anymore. It was nearly two in the morning before they dropped into bed.

Paul woke up at seven to take Luke to the park. He was relieved not to find Tyler there, though he would have liked to see Teddy. Returning home, he slept again. Then he spent a few hours arranging his room until it was time to leave for his shift at the food co-op.

His room was at the rear of the apartment. A curtain hung over the entrance, but Adrien had less privacy — the way to the front door led through his bedroom. As Paul made his way out a second time, Adrien

109

began to stir, and at the sudden motion Luke ran to the foot of the bed and trotted nervously back and forth, growling.

"What's wrong?" Adrien asked, sitting up.

"He's just upset from the move," Paul explained. "He probably misses the other dogs."

"Poor Luke. Do you miss your friends? Come here. Come on up here," Adrien coaxed, patting the bed. Luke jumped up, circled, and lay down.

"That's not a good idea," Paul warned.

"It's all right. I had a dog growing up. He always slept on my bed. It might comfort him to have somebody to curl up with."

"It's just going to be hard to break him of the habit if you change your mind."

But Adrien had already returned to his cocoon of faded bedding, one hand stretched across Luke's neck. "I won't," he said. "This is nice."

Adrien was waiting for him outside the food co-op when his shift ended, with Luke in tow.

"Thanks for taking Luke out," he said, "but — I'm on my way to Mass."

"It's okay. We'll wait outside."

"For forty-five minutes?"

"Sure. It's a nice night."

"Suit yourself," Paul said, and shrugged.

The church wasn't far away. The Haitian Mass had just ended, and groups of Creole-speaking worshippers exited as they approached.

"Oh, I've always wanted to come to one of the French services here," Adrien exclaimed, peering into the interior of the church. "How often do they have them?"

"Once each on Saturday and Sunday," Paul answered. "Go in, if you like. I can hold Luke for a few minutes if you want to look around."

"No thanks. You go in. We'll wait out here."

"You really don't have to, you know," Paul said. The warning was meant as much for himself as Adrien. "Stay or go, it's all the same to me."

But Adrien wouldn't be dissuaded. "I've got a few errands to run. I'll do those, and by the time I come back you'll be finished. If not, it's pretty nice here."

Felix and adauctus

"It is, isn't it?" Paul replied, tipping his head back to gaze overhead at the shaggy trees that grew around the church. In fact, he had chosen this parish precisely because of the grounds: a wilder assortment of flora surrounded the soot-blackened gothic building than graced the gardens of the area's other parishes. "If you're sure. If you change your mind, it's no problem. I'll see you at home."

With a small wave he went inside, pausing a moment to dip his hand in the holy water fount. How pleasant it was to be in church, he thought, where it was so dark and cool.

Without fanfare, a priest came onto the altar, trailed by two altar boys. All three began to move efficiently through the familiar ritual, almost indifferent to the few congregants scattered throughout the church. Their economy delighted Paul; they had obviously served together many times. He bowed his head to pray, and realized that the only thing that would please him as much as this Mass was finding Adrien and Luke waiting outside afterward.

Adrien's only errand had been to the liquor store on Fifth Avenue. At home they stayed up late drinking his favorite Portuguese wine and eating Paul's chick-pea and spinach curry. From a discussion of why Paul preferred St. Augustine's to the other neighborhood parishes, the talk turned to Christianity in general. Adrien asked what the current church teaching was on the events of the Inquisition. Paul said that the transcendent nature of Jesus and his message weren't diminished by the failings of the historical church, which was only an imperfect, earth-bound version of a perfect truth. Adrien, lapsed from Ethical Culture and now a casual Buddhist, made the case that the story of Jesus was really only a version of the more ancient sun-god myth. The choice of his birth date so near the winter solstice — when the sun began again to stay longer in the sky, thereby triumphing over darkness — certainly pointed to that interpretation. The fact that the timing of Easter also tied in with the celestial calendar clinched the argument. He talked about the Gnostics, who held very different ideas about Christ's humanity and human sexuality, among other things, from the church organization that ultimately prevailed. Gnosis meant "to know," whereas the form of Christianity that finally prospered, after much bloodshed, required blind belief, and that was why St. Jerome and the other conservative church

at home anywhere

fathers excommunicated the Gnostics.

At that point, Adrien seemed to realize that he hadn't given Paul a chance to respond to his remarks, and paused.

"You've really looked into this," Paul said, smiling. Then he quoted Galatians."There is neither Jew nor Greek, slave nor free, male nor female, for you are all one in Jesus Christ."

"What's that from?"

"The New Testament. It's one of the letters."

"I never heard that before. It's nice. You think the church will ever really accept it?"

"I'm hopeful. But it's going to take a long time and right now, though I hate to say it, Luke needs one more walk." Paul swayed when he stood up. "How much did we drink?" he said.

"Lots."

Paul thought of reminding Adrien, again, that he didn't need to come along, but decided not to. For a while they moved along the quiet streets in companionable silence. It soon became obvious that Adrien had continued the argument about the origins of Christianity inside his head, because he suddenly brought out that some scholars thought that Christ was probably a member of a Jewish sect called the Essenes, and had no idea of forming a new religion. Adrien had the books to support his views, despite the centuries-old and incredibly successful ongoing efforts of the official churches to stifle the information. When they returned to the apartment, he promised, Paul could read the evidence for himself and draw his own conclusions.

At home again, Paul removed Luke's leash and collapsed into a chair. But Adrien padded around the room in his socks, looking for one of the books he had mentioned. "There's one thing you have to see tonight; if you still disagree after you read this..."

"You don't have to find the book," Paul said, drowsily. "I believe you."

"It's on this shelf, I know it's here," Adrien protested, mistaking Paul's reluctance as impatience.

"I'm too drunk to read," Paul said. "I'm going to bed." He stood, but halfway to his small room at the rear of the apartment, he halted, and a moment later fell into Adrien's bed. After a little while Adrien came to stand alongside. "Don't get up," he said. "I'll use your bed tonight.

Felix and adauctus

That's if you don't mind." Eyes shut, Paul didn't stir. He could pretend to be asleep, overcome by wine. That way he could wait and examine his feelings before action made such reflection impossible.

Instead, opening his eyes, he reached out a hand and grasped one of Adrien's. It was like holding a small bird, fragile and trembling with life. "No, don't go. Stay here and hold me," he said.

They slept so late the next day that Paul missed the dog time in Prospect Park. After a breakfast of organic oatmeal, they made one loop of the park with Luke in tow and then Adrien took him to the Hadassah Thrift shop. At first, Paul was disappointed. Adrien's nearly new Birkenstocks must have been a fluke. Most of the merchandise at the store that day was very well used and hadn't been first quality to begin with. At one point, rounding a corner, he came upon a pair of work boots. Without thinking, he found himself examining the boots with a critical eye, and soon noticed the Timberland label. He almost wished Adrien would come alongside so he could impress him with a comment about the brand's questionable quality. He supposed he had something to thank Tyler for. His old roommate had taught him everything he knew about work boots.

He moved on. He had given up hope of finding anything when, just past the work boots, he came upon four pairs of shoes from the Egoiste shop, arranged atop a plastic trunk. Two pairs of wingtips, in black and brown, a pair of brogues, and a pair of patent leather slip-ons. Barely worn. They fit him almost perfectly. They were marked ten dollars a pair, but the woman at the cash register said that if Paul would take them all, he could have them for thirty. He tried to convey the significance of the find to Adrien, "These are three hundred dollar shoes," he said, "and I have such a hard time finding shoes that fit…" Adrien smiled and nodded, pleased at his pleasure, equally convinced that of course Paul had to buy them all: he could not expect a chance like this to come again.

He wore the black wingtips that evening to the restaurant. Got off the subway a stop early and skimmed along Madison Avenue. At the other restaurants he passed he noted that the tables had been set outside for the first time that year. He hoped they would open the sidewalk at Les Trois Oiseaux. Widening his stride he remembered how pleasant it was

at home anywhere

to come from the interior of the restaurant to the street as the sky finally darkened and the streetlights came on. Between seatings he'd stand with the other waiter under the open sky, the wingtips winking at the bottom of his long apron, and Adrien and Luke waiting up for him at home.

Mary Hoffman lives and works in Brooklyn, New York. Her stories have appeared in the *Gallatin Review* and the *Minetta Review*. She received a scholarship to study at the Norman Mailer Writers Center in the summer of 2010. In 2008 she won the New Rivers Press Many Voices Project Award for the stories in *At Home Anywhere*.